Bristol Short Story Prize Anthology

Volume Seven

Bristol Short Story Prize Anthology Volume 7

First published in 2014 by Tangent Books

Tangent Books
Unit 5.16 Paintworks
Bristol
BS4 3EH
0117 972 0645
www.tangentbooks.co.uk

Email: richard@tangentbooks.co.uk

ISBN: 978-1-910089-08-8

Cover designed by Rosanna Tasker
www.rosannatasker.com

Layout designed by Dave Oakley, Arnos Design
www.arnosdesign.co.uk

Printed and bound by ScandinavianBook.co.uk
Bloomsbury WC1H 9BB

A CIP catalogue record for this book is available from the British Library
www.tangentbooks.co.uk
www.bristolprize.co.uk

Contents

Introduction

Welcome to the seventh Bristol Short Story Prize anthology, and to a fantastic mix of stories that we hope will entertain, surprise, intrigue and engross you as much as they did the judges. Short fiction is having something of a moment, at last, and is being recognised and celebrated for the exciting form it is. This of course comes as no surprise to those of us who have been reading, writing and championing short stories for years, but it's satisfying to see one's enthusiasm reflected by publishers, online magazines and literary prizegivers. Some of the credit, I'd like to think, should go to the Bristol Short Story Prize for its energetic year-round support of the short story and for its commitment to publishing the twenty best entries from the competition: a significant publishing act of faith and one that every year reminds us of the enjoyment to be found in reading, and writing, short fiction.

This year's entries for the competition came from all round the world, nearly two and a half thousand of them from 65 countries. Heartfelt thanks should go to the tireless readers who presented the four judges with our longlist: forty hugely enjoyable and varied stories taking us across continents and countries, into cities, mountains, prairies and out to space, to the past and the future, into the worlds of the young and the very old. In judge Nikesh Shukla's words, "they gave us everything from the grand to the microscopic, the funny and strange and weird and wonderful."

Our shortlist was reached after a good deal of discussion and quite a few cakes. When one of us championed a story we felt had been unjustly overlooked, the others listened, and gave it another close reading. We talked about which stories moved us, made us laugh, kept us reading, about what worked well and what didn't quite come off. We agreed on the importance of endings: Sanjida O'Connell says: "Where I thought many of the stories fell down - in spite of beautiful prose or nuanced emotions - was in the final scene. As well as a cracking beginning a story needs a sound ending." Rowan Lawton adds that for her, a story needs to feel "complete in and of itself, leaving the reader thinking about the impact of what they have just read."

It was noticeable how many of the stories submitted had child or adolescent narrators, and we wondered if this was a reflection of literary trends, the state of the economy or the wider world. There were a number of stories featuring teenagers growing up in difficult circumstances or in children's homes; there were children who were caught up in the complexities of adult pain, separation or divorce; and many moments where young people faced a significant rite of passage. A child's point of view is surprisingly difficult to pull off convincingly, and what stood out for us in our first and second place stories was how effectively each created an authentic voice for their young narrators, as well as the originality of their settings. *The Art of Flood Survival* gives us the voice of a young servant in Bangladesh, a girl who knows just how the world works against those like her but who is canny and clear-eyed enough to seize the unexpected chance of a different future. In *Tata and Mama and Me* the young narrator's naivety and lack of understanding of the true circumstances in which he finds himself are given a terrible twist by our knowledge of the horror that forms the background to his games and drawing. *Debt*, in third place, is a tender but unsentimental description of family loyalty, where the relationship between two adult brothers is rooted in the events and brutalities of their childhood. All three end powerfully and left us with the sense that we had been in the hands of writers who had a sure sense of the story they wanted to tell.

We all owe a huge thank you to Joe Melia, who works incredibly hard all year round to make the Bristol Short Story Prize work so well. Big thanks should also go to all the 3rd year Illustration students at the University of the West of England who submitted cover designs for this anthology, and their course leaders, Chris Hill and Jonathan Ward. Rosanna Tasker's cover, selected from so many brilliant submissions, is a stunning piece of work – many congratulations to her.

It is great news for the Bristol Short Story Prize that Tangent Books have taken over the publication of the anthology from the sorely missed Bristol Review of Books magazine. To have the support of such an established and innovative publisher should ensure a healthy future for the competition.

As we came to the end of our judging session, we all realised what a pleasure and a privilege it had been to spend a long time talking seriously and enthusiastically about the craft of writing. So we'd like to thank all the writers who submitted stories to this year's prize for giving us that opportunity; to congratulate the three prizewinners and the seventeen others who feature with them in this anthology; and finally, to say: keep writing!

Sara Davies

1st Prize
Mahsuda Snaith

Mahsuda Snaith is a Leicester-based writer. She has won prizes in a number of national writing competitions including the *DreamUp! Monologue Competition* and The Asian Writer Short Story Competition 2012. Her first novel was recently a finalist in the *Mslexia* Novel Competition 2013. As well as short story and novel writing she is now working on her first full-length play. She is very fond of crochet (though not particularly good at it). www.mahsudasnaith.com.

The Art of Flood Survival

The flood comes overnight. I hear the *phlunkk! phlunnk!* as feet hit water. The English scream. Aiyh! Their voices clatter and slap my ears. "It does not flood in Syhlet," Mahmud told them. He had leant back on his chair, balancing his fat body on two legs as he stuffed paan leaf in the cave of his cheek. "We people have the sense to live on higher ground." Sense. Aiyh! As if floods have knowledge of such things. In the village of my birth we did not live on lower ground because we had no sense, we lived there because we had no choice. We learnt to survive the floods, to tie boats to iron posts, to build raised platforms for livestock. We made portable ovens to keep us fed in the worst of conditions and scaled the wire trunks of palm trees, keeping clear of danger while assessing the damage. Water can drown you but, if you give into its force, it can also keep you afloat.

But the English, they have no survival skills. They holler through the blue-black night even though it will make no difference. Even though this is Bangladesh, where screaming for help is as fruitful as asking the monsoon to stop bringing rain...

It is early morning when they arrive. The baby-taxi screeches a honking tune that cuts through the noise of the green rainfall. When we reach the gate the English are already outside. The girls are dressed in Western clothes; t-shirts and jeans like the boys in town but cut in a way that clings to the thighs. Their skin is a watery mud colour that makes them look sickly. The mother wears a salwar kameez; white scarf wrapped over her head, knot beneath her chin. You can hear the Bengali in the way she sighs but her body is wound up tight like a coiled rattlesnake.

There is no father with them. I wait a moment but when the taxi driver brings the last suitcase there is still no one.

"Rabeya!" cries Auntie snapping her hand towards the gate.

The rain smacks my face as I push the bars shut. When I run inside I stand behind the screen door where the English will not see me.

"Crazy crazy!" the mother is wailing.

She slaps her head, dropping down on Uncle's rosewood chair. Her round body deflates as she tells Auntie of the beggars at the airport, how they grabbed for their suitcases, had pulled at their clothes. They were mobbed she says, and nobody tells her she has forgotten her country already. That there is no mobbing in Bangladesh; just life.

Auntie tells me to tend to the chai in the kitchen. It has been brewing in a large steel pan with the lime green of cardamom pods and the deep mahogany of cloves and cinnamon floating on top. I sweeten it with four heaped spoons of sugar, stirring slowly as I add milk. The fiery smell hits the air, covering the sour stench of the rubbish heap in the back yard. When Auntie walks in she stops, chest inflating.

They are not my real Auntie and Uncle; they are my masters but they still let me call them this. Zubaida says this makes them good people. In her house they cry out 'Girl! Bring me the newspaper! Girl! Sweep the floors!' They treat her as if she is nothing more than an animal in the yard. Aiyh! No better than a dog on the street.

I ladle the chai into the teacups. They are white porcelain with pink roses and gold trim on the handles. I place them carefully across a steel tray. Auntie's hands shake as she lifts it, cups tinkling against the steel. I hope the guests will think this is because of age and not because she is worried about Mahmud arriving home earlier than Uncle.

I stay in the kitchen, turning the heat low beneath the pan, hearing the loud chatter of the two ladies as they reminisce about their childhood.

"*Rabeya!*" Auntie cries.

When I run into the main room, the English girls are limp on their seats. Their mud-water faces are now gaunt as goats as they swot lazily at clammy skin.

"*Coils,*" Auntie says.

I run to get the coils, placing them around the room before lighting the ends of their spiralling bodies. Smoke ripples up from their amber tails, spreading out into a fountain as it hits the ceiling. I watch the mosquitos fly into the fog before stumbling out. Their whining buzz clips to an end. If I had the power I would kill every mosquito in Bangladesh! With one flick of my hand I would shatter their needle mouths and burst their blood-filled bodies. Such tiny creatures yet still they are the greatest flood survivors of them all.

"Assalam alaikum."

I turn to see Uncle in the doorway. He stands in his long white kurta like the Great Egret standing in the tall grass of the paddy fields. There is much noise and touching of feet. Even the English girls show this respect. I run to the kitchen to bring out another cup of chai. When I come back Auntie passes it to Uncle, lifting the teacup by the saucer, hands no longer shaking.

Auntie tells me to sweep the girls' room. When I go in they are sitting on the bed, backs slumped against the brick. The younger girl is touching the screen of a thin silver box.

I try to be invisible to them because I do not want them to slap me the way Mahmud does. Auntie's slaps are short and sharp but Mahmud thumps so hard it makes me dizzy.

"What is your name?" asks one of the girls.

It is the older one. Her Bengali is weak but I do not tell her this.

"Rabeya," I say, staying squat to the floor.

I sweep the dust with a straw broom while the girl questions me. Where am I from? Where is my family? What are my jobs? Do I mind this work?

She speaks these questions with an easy smile and I think perhaps she is tricking me; that she will report me to Uncle. I tell her I am from a small village many miles outside of Syhlet. I have four sisters and two brothers.

"When do you see them?"

I pause, watching the straw twist side to side as I sweep.

"Before the last monsoon, maybe longer."

The younger girl looks up from her box. She says something but, aiyh!, her Bengali is worse than her sisters. I thought these English were well educated but they cannot even speak their own language.

"She's asking if you miss them," the older one says.

I stop sweeping. I think about my baby brothers and how I carried them around the village like monkeys carry their young. I think of Zubaida, just one year older than me, and how she hollered when she had to return to her master's house. How she clung onto my arm as Abba pulled her to the rickshaw, wailing and shouting my name as if it was me who decided she should go. Abba grabbed hold of her hair and yanked so hard she had no choice but to let go. I ran inside with tears in my eyes to find Amma plucking the feathers off a dead duck. She did not look up but simply wiped the sweat from her forehead.

"No," I say. "I do not miss them."

I think this will be the end of it but the girl now asks my age. I shrug. When I do this the younger one leans closer to her sister and whispers in her ear.

"My sister thinks you are eight or nine," the older one says.

I think of the charity school in the village and how they taught us numbers, pushing pink chalk in large loops across slate, singing the sequence out loud.

"Eight," I say. "Yes I am eight."

The girls are quiet. I leave the room quickly before they think of more questions.

I help Auntie gut the ilish fish and fetch the heavy pots into the kitchen. I am small but I am strong and lift two or three pots, no problem. Aiyh! I am probably stronger than a boy!

Auntie takes the edge of her knife and skims the scales off the fish in one straight sweep. The small discs shimmer as they make a silver-pink pile on the floor. I look at the goggling eyes of the ilish, wondering if it saw the net before the fishermen caught it.

There is a clatter at the front gate. For a moment I think it is Uncle returning from the masjid, but then I hear the rev of a motorbike.

Auntie's face tightens as she looks at me.

"Chai."

I run over to the steel pan, tilting it over as I scoop out what is left. When I walk into the main room Mahmud is sitting on a chair with legs spread wide, thumbs hooked into pockets. His black moustache is waxed into points like a film villain. Mahmud preens and combs his moustache every day. I believe the closest he feels to love is his adoration of that gleaming cockroach.

"Of course my dear cousins," he says as I bring him the chai. "It is so good to see you."

He wiggles his head and gives them his phann stained grin, leaving me to stand with the teacup in my hand. The mother is wearing a leaf green sari. She sits in her chair, body loose with the heat. The girls are fatigued and do not look at their cousin. I think this makes them wise.

Auntie walks in and suddenly Mamud's voice grows loud.

"How are you liking our great country of Bangladesh?"

The girl's nod but do not smile while their mother fans her face with a newspaper. I see Auntie's brow wrinkle. She wants to reprimand Mahmud for his lateness but instead mops the sweat from her forehead with the end of her sari.

"They have not left the house yet," she says.

Mahmud's eyes widen as though she has told him they have not eaten for three days.

"This is terrible!" he cries. "Bangladesh is the most beautiful country in all of Asia! Our tea plantations are very famous. Of course your cousin Mahmud will take you."

The girls' eyes lift while Auntie's become hard.

"They are here for business only. There is no point dragging them around during monsoon."

Mahmud grins at his cousins.

"What is the point of business if there is no *pleasure*."

The girls look at each other, then lower their heads.

Mahmud's phone buzzes and he leaves the room. When he returns he is wiggling his head and grinning.

"I have spoken to my friend. We will go to the plantation tomorrow. It will be very cheap."

Auntie begins to protest but the mother stops her.

"He is right," she says. "My children should see the beauty of our country."

When Auntie marches back into the kitchen Mahmud sits down. He swings back on the chair.

"How are you liking your cousin Mahmud and his moustache?"

He twiddles the ends of his whiskers. They all laugh.

The next day the girls put on a salwar kameez and cover their heads with their dupattas. Even still, the taxi driver will see their easy smiles and treble the rates.

The older one smiles at me as I sweep the room, but I look away. She comes to me, placing a finger on my chin, and turns my face to look at her. For a moment I think she will slap me but instead she whispers.

"You must not be sad. We shall bring back photos."

I do not understand this word.

"*Foh-toe?*" I say.

She takes out a red box from her bag and holds it in front of her. When she presses the button a light pops from the corner. She turns the box around and, aiyh!, I see my face looking back at me with surprise.

"I am inside?" I ask, tapping the screen.

"No no," says the older sister. "It is just a photo."

"*Foh-toe.*"

She laughs and I laugh too. The other sister seems pleased and joins in. Mahmud hears all this cheerfulness and is quick to investigate. When he strides in I squat low and begin to sweep. I glance up as he takes hold of the box and twiddles his moustache.

"Yar yar, this is a very good camera."

He looks it over as though he is an expert when all he has is a mobile phone, not slim and silver like the girls, but thick and black like a sun-scorched cow turd. He sees me scowling at him and, even though I know he wants to slap me, he grins at his cousins and tells them the baby taxis have arrived.

I watch them leave through the bars of the gate. The rain is light but the girls carry big umbrellas until they are inside the vehicles. Mahmud holds his arm out for the mother and sweet-talks her all the way to the baby taxi. I look down the street at the bougainvillea trailing over white painted walls, stray dogs lying lazy in the sun, school children riding their bikes through rust coloured mud. I lock the padlock on the gate. When I look up I see the girls waving from the baby taxi. It is only when I look behind me that I realise they are waving at me.

As I squat to wash the dishes I think of the children riding home from school. The boys in their shorts and shirts, the girls wearing pinafore dresses, hair oiled and plaited in black ropes on either side of their head. The water bubbles as it hits the stone and I carry on scrubbing until every fishbone is washed down the drain.

The lady from the charity wanted me to go to a school here in Syhlet. She came to the house and cupped her hand around my cheek, asking me questions about what village I came from. I wanted to tell her about the charity school back home, how they taught me to read and write and how I was always top of my class! But I knew that I could not say these things in front of Uncle. So he spoke for me instead, chin raised high as though insulted to be asked in the first place.

Later I heard Mahmud tell Uncle there was no use educating a child who would only be a housegirl. He tossed his hand in the air.

"It will give her airs and graces," he said.

Uncle listened and, for the first time I have witnessed, agreed with Mahmud. Uncle is older than me and wiser but, aiyh! I wish he had not.

Zubaida told me of a housegirl, just like us, who attended a charity school and learnt art, dancing, reading and writing. This same girl went to her master asking for more pay because she was now a skilled worker. I asked Zubaida if she was beaten badly for this but Zubaida said no.

"He agreed! Can you believe it Rabeya?"

Aiyh! I could not.

I did not fight and kick the day I was sent here to work, but I cried so wildly that everyone stopped their street work to look at us. When we were outside the house Abba grabbed hold of me, telling me he would beat me if I carried on with my wailing. I should be grateful, he said, the money I would send home would feed the whole family. Wasn't this better than being dumped on the streets and left to beg for my living? Or being married off to a fifty-year-old man who would treat me like a slave and worse besides? I should be grateful for this job and respect my employees or they would kick me out. I must not tell them I could read and write or they would think me too educated. It was better that I appeared stupid to them.

So I hid this from my masters and they have been happy with my stupidity. It is like Mahmud says, there is no use educating a child who will only be a housegirl.

The sky is sapphire-black when Mahmud and the English return. They walk through the gate with wide grins and a rumbling laughter that echoes through the rain. When they are inside I see the mother search through her purse and place taka notes in Mahmud's hand. He protests, but only for a moment.

Later, the girls usher me to their room.

"Look," says the older girl, holding her photobox in front of me.

On the screen I see pictures of green hills rolling out for miles, ladies carrying woven baskets filled with freshly picked leaves on their heads. I ask the girls if they saw tigers. Their eyes widen and they say *nooo!*

Our talking stops when we hear Mahmud shouting from the main room. "Allah!" he cries. "You cannot expect things to be easy like England. Your papers will be lost, they will charge you twice the fee!"

We hear the mumble of the mother's voice.

"Trust me auntie!" Mahmud says. "I know people who can help with this problem. It will take one day, maximum."

Mahmud does not return for three days.

The mother begins to complain about the heat and her back pain, pacing the house up and down. When she speaks with Uncle and Auntie she is tense, her words sharp. Even her daughters are afraid, sneaking off to their room to whisper in words I cannot understand.

They no longer speak to me. I forgive them for this because, when the time comes, I know they will help me.

When Mahmud returns it is after nightfall. He is wet with rain and stinks of beer. He makes so much noise singing and banging into furniture that everyone stumbles out of their beds. I follow the girls as they step into the main room, staying crouched down in the corner so he cannot see me. Since the other children married and left, Uncle has controlled his son single-handedly but even he cannot tame a drunk Mahmud.

"You must not worry," Mahmud tells the mother. "You will get your money back twofold. You must give me time, yar?"

"I want it now!" she says, slapping her hands together. "We have airplane seats booked for tomorrow."

Mahmud shrugs his shoulders.

"I will forward you the money."

He lifts his hand as though this is the end of the matter.

Auntie steps forward. The moonlight hits her eyes and I see they are wide, red lines weaving through the white. She begins chopping her hand towards Mahmud.

"Fool boy! You have gambled it away! You have drunk it down the drain! You are a devil boy Mahmud and one of these days you will be killed for your sins!"

Mahmud's eyes grow as wide as his mother's. He stands straight, his top lip curling back beneath his cockroach moustache.

"You will ruin my name old woman?"

His voice creeps higher with each word.

"You will make a fool of me in front of my English relatives?!"

Mahmud swings his hand up. His eyes are so fierce that I know the blow will send Auntie to the floor.

"Aiyh!" Uncle cries.

The noise is enough to keep Mahmud's hand hovering in the air.

When Uncle speaks again his voice is dry and rattling.

"Do not bring any more shame on this house Mahmud," he says. "Allah knows I will not allow it!"

Mahmud looks at his father, then at his English cousins who have horror flickering through their eyes. He turns to go, the clattering of the gate soon followed by the rev of his motorbike.

The girls toss on their mattress and cannot sleep. I creep to the side of their bed, hooking my fingers on the edge of their sheets.

"You are going back to England tomorrow?"

For a while, all I hear is the rain beating on the roof and the howling of wind.

"Yes."

It is the older one that speaks. I see the roundness of her cheek glow in the soft moonlight. I squeeze on tighter to the sheets, feeling the moth-eaten holes between my fingers.

"Will you take me?"

The rain goes *da-rum, da-rum* inside me, filling me up like a barrel. I wait, wondering if she has not heard.

"I shall be a very good servant," I say.

Her body curls tight, sheets rippling around her legs.

"We do not have servants in England."

I frown and look back at her cheek.

"Will you take me anyway?"

The wind howls like a tortured banshee. I watch her jaw clench and think it is from fear, but when she speaks again her voice is stern and sharp.

"No Rabeya. Now please leave us alone."

...The flood comes overnight. When the waters rise I tie the skirt of my kameez around my waist and climb out of the back window.

As the English scream and Auntie and Uncle try to make sense of the flood I scramble up the trunk of a starfruit tree. I hear Auntie calling all the names of her children until Uncle reminds her it is only Mahmud who lives with them now.

"Mahmud!" she cries. "Where is my dear boy Mahmud?"

She carries on calling his name even when they are through the gate, the English following in a neat line as they wade through the water.

She does not call for me. But then, I did not expect her to.

I pull a starfruit from the branch of the tree and bite into its rubbery skin. The flesh is sweet and fragrant. Soon, the noise of Auntie's wailing fades, replaced with the drumming of rainfall. She thinks her son has perished in the waters but Mahmud is a mosquito. He will profit from this flood just like those biting beasts do; making love to the still water, laying their eggs within. As the water rises so will his numbers, a thousand little Mahmud's swarming for the nearest prey.

I watch the sun rise over the flooded city. The red shimmers across the water like flames in a rubbish pyre. Far away I see men in lungis riding rickshaws and the bare chests of boys as they wash themselves from the waist up. I look over the pastel painted houses and palm trees shooting up to the sky and think this must be what the Great Egret sees when she is flying to her next destination. I will be like the bird; I will fly from this place, the wind rushing through my feathers with wings outstretched.

I hear the rumble of an engine. When I rub my eyes I see an orange rescue boat cutting through the water. A rippled tail fans out from behind. There is an art to flood survival. The art is to prosper from it. I shout at the boat, my cries so loud that the men look up and cut their engine dead.

As I climb down the trunk I think of my story.

I will tell them I am from a good family, washed away in the floods.

I will tell them I am well educated, that I know how to read and write.

I will tell them I am a survivor.

2nd Prize
Claire Griffiths

Claire Griffiths was born and raised in the village of Aboyne
in north-east Scotland. She completed an MA in Creative
Writing at the University of East Anglia, Norwich in 2009,
graduating with Distinction. She currently divides her time
between London and Norwich, teaching Creative Writing
and Literature modules at the UEA and the University of
Westminster, while she completes a scholarship-funded PhD
in Creative and Critical Writing. Her short stories have been
featured in several print publications and broadcast on BBC
Radio 4. *Tata and Mama and Me* is taken from her near-
complete debut novel *The Gallery*, which focuses on artworks
produced by Auschwitz prisoners during World War II.

Táta and Máma and Me

When I step out of the big shed the sunshine gets in my eyes and they go blind. I blink hard, and when the black circles clear I see a group of the other children in the yard. They are playing 'Blockade: *Aktion*'. I know this because the older ones have guns, which means that they are the Guards. They are not real guns, of course – they are only made of air – but I can see them like they are real and I know the big kids can too. Their right hands curl under their armpits while their left hands hold the muzzles. They keep them hoisted as they search the Family Camp: inside and all around the other big sheds.

I want to join in the game because it looks fun, but I have work to do. I carry my sheet of paper carefully because Máma says it is the last piece. I hold it out in front of me the way I used to carry the tea tray for her when we lived in the proper house in Prague. I imagine that Máma's best crockery is set out on top: the cups with gold leaves around the rim and a different animal on each saucer. I liked the fox best and the badger second. The blue pencil in the pouch of my smock is the sugar spoon that Máma would plop into the chest pocket of my smart brown shirt.

"Now we are ready for them!" she would say.

As we walked into the Parlour Room, the ladies from Máma's prayer group would look up – all at once, like birds that have spotted fallen crumbs – from the parochets or Torah mantles that they would be sewing for synagogue.

"Such a big strong boy you have, Eliška," they'd exclaim, as my arms wobbled under the weight of the tray.

The table in the Parlour Room had a smell of clean boots that always tickled my nose. I would set the tray down on the white coverlet that Máma sewed herself; the one made of holes and strings with a pattern of orange flowers. As Máma poured the tea, the prayer group ladies would lean in, their long fingers pecking – slowly at first then faster and faster – at a plate of rugelachs in the centre of the tray. I would stand by Táta's armchair, picking at the loose threads where Pippi-Cat used to scratch, my eyes trained hopefully on the shrinking mound of rolled-up triangles. Sometimes they would be nutty inside; sometimes filled with apple jam. Best of all was Máma's special syrup that tasted like perfume smells.

But there will be no reward this afternoon for the big strong boy: no *putt-putt* sound as the pastry breaks and turns to mush inside my mouth; no hot filling turning the top of my tongue to sand. Sighing, I climb onto a bench next to one of the outside tables. I find a section of the wooden surface that does not have bird shit on it and put the paper down. Taking out my blue pencil, I tuck my legs under my bottom and wonder what I should draw. But all I can think of is the rugelachs.

Pavel comes over. He is Czech like me, but much older – fourteen at least. Máma says our families went to the same synagogue before we were moved to Theresienstadt and then here, but I do not remember. I am scared of him when I am not on his team for games, but in real life he is alright.

Pavel is playing a Guard; he is one of the older boys so he always plays a Guard. He stamps on the ground and stands to attention.

"Have you seen ze vun zey call Hanuš?" he says. His German accent is very good.

"No," I answer.

"*Nein,*" he corrects.

"Sorry – *nein.*"

"Vot about Hanna? Or Miroslav or any of ze ozer leettle vuns?"

"*Nein – ich…habt…nicht.*" I am proud of myself for having remembered so much German. I must tell Táta later.

Pavel does not seem impressed with my German. He bends into a half-squat and raises his gun.

"You are sure?" he says. "You are not on ze side of ze Leettle Jews, are you?"

I am worried now; Pavel is taking the game very seriously.

"No – *nein.* I am not playing. I am drawing."

The gun stays where it is: "Vot for?"

"Máma wants me to make a special picture." The words sound stupid in my mouth. "Táta is sick and needs it to help him feel better."

"*Pisher*" Pavel snorts, forgetting to be German for a moment. He runs off.

I am embarrassed: I am not a pisher; I am a big strong boy. And I don't want to make a stupid picture; I want to play 'Blockade: *Aktion*' and hunt the Little Jews and rob their things and eat. I want rugelachs and plum dumplings and poppy-seed pirishkes, all dripping in prune butter. I want everything.

If I chase after Pavel maybe he will let me join the game. But I am only eight, so it is not certain he will let me be a Guard. I look at the group: they are stalking in a star formation now, their backs to each other, guns pointed outwards. Gerta is one of the Guards and she is eight years old. But no one says no to Gerta because she is built of bricks and likes to kick boys. Hanuš is also eight Pavel said he is hiding which means he is a Little Jew. But then Hanuš is a little jew; his Máma used to say he did not grow properly because she hugged him too much when he was born (I am not sure that this is true). But I am not nearly as big as Gerta even though I am taller than Hanuš. It is too risky, I decide; I don't want to be a Little Jew. Probably it is best that I don't play anyway; Táta is very sick. That much was clear this morning when I repeated the hysterical joke I overheard from a real-life SS guard to him. It must have been hysterical because the SS man laughed for ages after he told it.

"What do you call a thousand Jews on a train, Táta?" I said to the figure hunched up on the wooden bunk.

But he did not make a guess, not even when I said it again. He just carried on shivering.

"Your father does not need this now," Máma said, swatting me towards the door as though I were an annoying fly.

I tried to explain to her that if he heard the punch line – 'Fucked!' – just the way the SS man had said it, then maybe Táta would laugh too and wouldn't shiver anymore. But she only nodded her head like she does when she is not really listening, and handed me the paper.

"Go and draw something," she said. "It will make Táta feel better."

Sometimes it is a lot of responsibility, being so excellent at art.

But all of this thinking has made an idea appear in my head: I will draw Táta. I am best at drawing people, after all. And if I draw Táta standing up and smiling perhaps it will encourage him to stop lying in bed being miserable.

I start with Táta's outline, the way that *Slečna* Marianne has taught us to during our lessons here. I do his legs first, nice and skinny, pressing gently because the paper is thin and the pencil can easily pop right through it. The legs come out wobblier than I would like but it makes Táta look more ill, which is realistic. I do his shirt next and then his hands – up in the air, like he is cheering because he is getting better.

I do the face last because *Slečna* Marianne says always do it last she is always right. I leave a gap at the top of Táta's head so I can draw his cap without a line going through it. 'That is very clever art, Jiří,' I imagine my teacher saying, her pretty brown curls bobbing at the sides of her head.

I start to colour in the rectangle of Táta's coat. Normally it is irritating only having a blue pencil and greyish paper, but today it is lucky – Táta's clothes will be true-to-life. I colour a blue stripe up, then a blue stripe down, then a blue stripe up and a blue stri–

Wheeeeeeeh – and here are the Little Jews! They dart around the corner of the farthest away shed; past a surprised Gerta, whose eyes are as wide as those of the bug-eyed prisoners that live on the other side of the fence. Pavel is in pursuit, his gun up and his face red.

"Suvvender you leettle sheets!" he screams.

Most of the Jews stay in a group because they are stupid, so it is easy for the Guards to surround them. They put their hands up and drop to their knees. But four or five break off and keep on running. They are even more stupid; the Guards put up their guns up and – *dugga-dugga-dugga* – the Little Jews fall. A couple stagger a few steps before dropping while another crawls a short distance before releasing a final gurgle. The Guards cheer: they win again!

But wait – someone is still standing! It is Alfred: scrawny, scabby, seven-year-old Alfred. Somehow the bullets have missed him or bounced off him because there he is, over by the electric fence. He does not flinch, even as Pavel walks towards him, firing off round after round. The Little Jew waits until he has everyone's attention.

"I give myself to *Hashem!*" he shouts, throwing himself against the wire.

Alfred's body shudders violently as electricity does a victory dance through his veins. He collapses to the ground, still shaking.

All is silent as both the Guards and Jews stare, open-mouthed. Alfred remains where he is, still now and lying face down on the earth. Pavel begins to clap and whoop – and slowly all the others join in. "Bravo!" they cry. "Bravo!"

Alfred stands up, wipes some dirt from his smock and takes a bow. His grin could not be wider if he stuck his forefingers in each side of his mouth and pulled. I applaud too because it really was fine acting; I truly believed the fence had been turned on early.

Alfred struts over to re-join the group and I turn back to the drawing. My heart thumps when I realise that all of the excitement has made me puncture the paper: Táta looks like he has a bullet hole going right through his chest. I am angry at first, but then I decide it is okay because Táta does have holes in his clothes. I push the pencil through the paper a few more times to show it is intentional. 'A fine save, Jiří!' my imaginary *Slečna* Marianne says, clapping her soft white hands together.

The guards – the real SS ones – never have holes in their clothes. Their coats and their trousers and their boots and their hats are always clean and perfect. I like the jackets they wear best and the waist belts second. The buttons on the jackets sparkle when the sun hits them, and the black belts make everything look tucked in and smart. My clothes, however, are like Táta's; I would much rather have German clothes.

But this has given me another idea – 'A brilliant idea!' my imaginary Marianne cries – I will draw another person alongside Táta: me. Only in the picture I will have nice clothes and this will make Táta feel good.

Drawing my outline is more difficult than doing Táta's, because I am not drawing from real life. It takes a lot of concentration to get my coat right, but I manage because of my talent – 'Such talent!' admires Marianne. I decide I will do the trousers next then a big pair of boots.

"Hi Jiří."

It is Alena. She is thirteen and has lumps on her chest already, which means none of the girls like her but all the boys do. Hanuš brags that she showed him her lumps once, in exchange for the flowered headscarf that was all he had left of his Máma. Alena uses it as a handkerchief.

Some of the boys whistle when they see she has stopped by my table, but she ignores them.

"Pavel said you are drawing a picture," she says, tugging her long blonde plait. "What are you drawing it with?"

"Pencil," I mumble, keeping my head down because my face is hot.

"I can see that, *nebbish*! But what colour?"

I don't like it when Alena calls me a loser; my cheeks get redder.

"Blue."

"Am I in the picture?" she says, leaning over the table to take a closer look.

"No."

"Why not – don't you think I would make a good subject?"

All I can think is that if I turn my head now I might be able to see down her vest.

"You didn't want to play Blockade with us?" she says, standing up straight again like she read my thought.

"No," I say. My throat is dry because it knows that I am lying.

"Why not?"

I don't want to tell Alena the truth like I did Pavel. I don't want her to think I am a *pisher*.

"It's boring."

She laughs and I can see inside her mouth; it is pink and soft and wet.

"I think it's boring too," she says. "It was much better in Theresienstadt – there were more places for the Jews to hide. Auschwitz only has the barracks."

I don't know what to say, so I carry on drawing.

"Why don't we play something else?" Alena suggests. "Look – they are doing Hats Off over there."

She is right: on the other side of the fence a line of prisoners are kneeling on the ground, their hats by their sides. Three SS march up and down the row, shouting at them and spitting on the ground. One of the guards has badges on his chest: a black cross and two big coins. I wonder if he will use the coins to buy his dinner later. My stomach rumbles.

"We could play Hats Off," Alena says, her voice suddenly low and breathy. "We could go behind the barracks – I'll even let you be the Guard."

I push my bottom lip in front of my top one and try to blow air onto my face, but it goes straight up my nose. I want to say yes, very badly. But I look at the picture of Táta and at his wobbly legs. And I remind myself that Alena is not to be trusted.

"I have more important things to do," I mumble.

She laughs: "Suit yourself."

As she walks away, hips swinging, the wind picks up her skirt enough that I can see the backs of her knees.

It is only as I finish the boots and sit back to consider the picture that I see I have made a mistake. I have forgotten the second most important of *Slečna* Marianne's rules for drawing: scale. 'Silly Jiří!' I hear her scold, as though she looks over my shoulder now at Táta and his twice-the-size son. 'You let yourself get distracted by a girl – that is no good.'

I frown at the picture; I hate it. I hate that it means I cannot play games or go behind the barracks with Alena. But most of all I hate it because I got it wrong, which means I am no good for anything – not even art. And worst of all, I cannot start again because there is no more stupid paper.

I look at the other children because I cannot look at the drawing anymore. The Guards have finished pretend-plundering the big sheds and are sitting down to feast on imaginary Jew-food: air-matzo ball soup, air-potato kugel, air-challah – yum, yum, yum, they scoff it all down. Of all the Little Jews, only Alfred has been permitted to join the feast. This is a Big Deal: it means he will be allowed to be a Guard next time and no seven-year-old has ever got to be a Guard before. The rest of the younger children kneel in a line, their arms linked together as though tied, watching the Guards fake-eat. This makes me even angrier: if I were not Jewish, I could have all the food I wanted and all the paper too.

Máma once told me that I am only Jewish because she is; that if Táta had married a non-Jewish girl I would have been just Czech. I try not to be angry at her for this, but I do think it makes her selfish – and all the other mothers here selfish too. When I grow up I will marry a nice non-Jewish girl so our children can have food and paper, and pencils in lots of colours.

But – another idea! Why can I not be grown-up in the picture? That way I should be taller than Táta, and that will make it all ok. 'Good, Jiří – the artist is back now!' Marianne says, ruffling my hair so my head goes all wooshy. I draw some extra wrinkles on Táta, to show how very old he is. Then I draw a badge on my chest – a big cross, just like the guard had – to show that I am, after all, the best ever at art.

I start colouring in my clothes: blue jacket, blue trousers; blue boots. I pay special attention, determined not to let Marianne down again. If my clothes are to look perfect then I must be neat and stay inside the lines. But only having one colour is not ideal; it is hard to tell where the trousers end and the boots begin.

I am so hungry now that it hurts. There must still be a long time to go before dinner because the sun has not started to dip yet and I cannot hear the low hum that means the fence has been turned on for the night. It does not help that the big chimneys are puffing out smoke again, making everything smell of meat.

The Guards must be real-life hungry too; they are getting more and more involved in their game. Some have scooped up dirt and mixed it with spit to make little cakes to coo over. Others are chewing on sticks as though they are chicken bones. Rudi is on his hands and knees, jerking his head as though he is an animal tearing flesh off a corpse.

The Little Jews are bored now of just sitting in their line. One by one, the younger children unlink their arms and assemble at the other end of the yard. They begin a game of Electric Fence, daring each other to run up and touch the wire. They throw sticks and rocks at it to reassure each other it is still safe.

I imagine one of them putting their hand on the fence and getting zapped. I wonder what the other kids would do: would they cry and scream or would they run over and tear the barbecued body to bits? I imagine tucking into a warm, dripping shin bone and my mouth floods with saliva.

If our parents saw us eating the child, would they would tell us off or join in too? Probably there would be a rule about not eating humans just like there is for pigs. I once asked Máma: if a pig walked through the camp right now, would she kill it and feed it to me and Táta? She said no.

I am getting angry again: our adults are so stupid. They say ridiculous things about hugging babies so much they do not grow; about having to be Jewish just because our mothers are; about silly pictures making people feel better. But they would not eat a piece of meat if it walked right past them or fell off the fence.

German adults are smart and that is why they are the bosses. They are clean, they wear nice clothes, they have guns and they eat all the time – any meat they like. I bet they wouldn't even blink at eating a fence-fried child if they were hungry.

I have another good idea: Máma should be in the picture too. She will have her best dress on and she will be cheering because Táta is getting better. But I will give her a pig nose, even though it is not nice, because I am feeling mean. 'Careful, Jiří,' Marianne warns, but this time I ignore her.

The crunch of the gravel tells me that Alena has returned. She has her hands behind her back.

"Jiří, what do you think? I have a pencil for you – it is red! You only have blue, don't you? Think of what you could do with red too."

I do think of it: red mouths for Táta and Máma and me; and, if I press lightly, pink faces too; and my uniform – a red band around the sleeve of my jacket and a red stripe above my badge. I reach out my hand but Alena steps away.

"Uh-uh. You have to come behind the barracks with me if you want it."

"Why not here?"

"Oh Jiří," she says, batting her eyelashes. "You know if the other boys see me giving you a present they will get jealous."

My eyes narrow: Alena is not to be trusted, after all. I know this because I alone know the real story of her and Hanuš – the one he made me promise not to tell the other children. When Alena led him around the corner of the big shed, Gerta was waiting there to beat him up. Alena took the headscarf.

"Let me see the pencil," I say.

Alena shakes her head, scratching circles in the dirt with her shoe.

"Only if you come behind the barracks with me. If you bring your blue pencil too, I will let you draw me. However you like – naked, even. Wouldn't you like that?"

Something in my brain pings: so that is what she is after.

"No, I wouldn't like that, Alena," I say, clenching my fist around my precious pencil. "I wouldn't like that because you are an ugly *nafka*."

Alena jumps back like I have shot her.

"What did you say?"

Power surges through my body like I am the one who has been zapped by the fence.

"I said you are a whore, Alena – just like that mother of yours who *stups* SS men for food."

"Bastard!" Alena starts swiping at her nose and eyes with her sleeve.

I watch her sprint all the way back to the barracks, past the older children who have finally given up their feast in favour of a game of Gas Chamber. They stand solemnly around the edge of a pit, taking turns to throw rocks in. The thrower makes choking noises while the others hiss.

I am still flushed with feeling: I am the Guard and I am victorious! I pick up my pencil again and draw myself a helmet and some shining buttons. I add a belt with a rectangular buckle, and two big coins to the badges on my chest. Finally I sketch my gun, pointing directly at Táta and Máma to show them that I am the boss now.

Only the faces are left to do: I decide Máma will look scared – O mouth – because she knows I am angry with her. But Táta will be smiling – U mouth – because he is proud of his big strong German son.

'It is your finest ever picture, Jiří!' my *Slečna* Marianne tells me, planting a kiss on my cheek.

3rd Prize
Tom Vowler

Tom Vowler is a novelist and short story writer living in south west England. His debut collection, *The Method* (Salt), won the Scott Prize in 2010, and his novel *What Lies Within* (Headline) received critical acclaim. He is co-editor of the literary journal *Short Fiction* and an associate lecturer in Creative Writing at Plymouth University, where he's completing a PhD looking at the role of the editor in fiction. His second novel, *That Dark Remembered Day* (Headline), was published in early 2014. More at www.tomvowler.co.uk

Debt

I pick him up from the airport. My younger brother, home under the cover of night to make good everything again.

- You look all skinny, he says. Jane not feeding you?

As we release each other, I offer to take his bag but he ignores me.

- I lucked out with the cabin crew, he says. They used to be up for a bit of flirting; came with the job.

I picture my brother attaching himself like a limpet to some poor jet-lagged woman, who in a bar or at a party would extract herself with a weary refrain, but who, at 28,000 feet, has no enduring escape routes.

- Do you ever have a day off? I say.

- The world is what it is, little brother. Despite the year and a bit I have on him, he's called me this since bulking out in his late teens. You should come over and stay, he says. Taste some Mediterranean delights.

Over was in the hills outside Marbella, Conor's home for the last four years, chosen when run-ins with Dublin's petty criminals progressed to something potentially mortal. There had been no time for goodbyes, our mother phoning me in a panic when she realised he'd left in the small hours one New Year's Eve.

I'd long since moved out – another kind of fleeing, I suppose – a vestige of respectability found teaching music at a failing Galway comprehensive.

Far enough away to visit if I had to, but with an infrequency that suited me. My departure meant our sister was now the sole provider of nurturance to a mother who measured the day's passing in alcoholic rather than temporal units. Our father, not much good at life either, at least had the sense to get out before his own tyranny imprisoned him, leaving the day before my fifteenth birthday. Our mother's judgement was typically understated. You'll all leave in the end, she said.

- Maybe I'll come over in the holidays, I say.

- Bring some crisps with you; they have no idea about crisps.

Conor lights a cigarette, opens the car window a crack. He smells of something I can't place, the odour of a foreign life. A good life, I imagine, though I know nothing of its particulars.

- Things working out for you over there? I say.

- Ah, you know, sun, sea and all that. I play golf every morning. Can you believe it? I used to hate those pricks with their polo shirts and their buggies. Now I'm one of them.

- You're right, I don't believe it.

- No good, though. I hook everything. Grip's too strong, apparently.

I imagine the club in his hands, absent of all finesse.

- You got work? I say.

- When I want it.

- Legal?

- Hey, come on. I've been back five minutes. What is this?

- I'm interested, that's all.

He turns the radio on, scans through the stations, settling on some whiny rock anthem that sees him drum the dashboard, which should annoy me but somehow doesn't. The road south is quiet at this time of night, allowing me to watch a chalky moon sat large over the city. I think to say I'm happy he's back, how it's good to see him, but just drive instead.

- You had this long? Conor says, making a play of checking the seatbelt.
- Couple of years.
- And you haven't written it off yet? I'm impressed.
- Funny.

The last time I saw my brother his foot had a man's head fixed to the floor. I'd come home for the holidays and he'd taken me on a tour of his latest nocturnal haunts – degenerate places in the north of the city – and I soon got the sense it was for my benefit, his illegitimate world proudly paraded, as if to make the point his was a successful life despite the absence of an honest vocation. As one by one he introduced me to men I sensed were best avoided, I imagined the inverse, of my showing him round the school, meeting colleagues in the staffroom, eating in the canteen. Midway through the evening an argument broke out in a nightclub, an acquaintance of Conor's unable to appease a group of disgruntled customers, my brother approaching with quiet relish as he took out the most vocal of them. Go in quick and hard, his way. For weeks, whenever the Head annoyed me, I imagined employing such decisive conflict resolution. I remember before our father left, he told me he'd never have to worry about Conor, that he would always be able to look after himself, the implication being that I couldn't.

In the absence of an obvious authority figure, Conor's passage through adolescence became progressively turbulent, although when I left for the west coast, his criminal record remained modest, boasting little more than vandalism, a caution for shoplifting and possession of some Class B. Charm and good fortune, as much as his physique, seemed to insulate him from the more extreme elements of retribution his lifestyle yielded. Until, that was, the wrong people were crossed, liberties taken where none were tolerated. According to our sister, he lost several kilograms of Columbia's finest in a bungled deal, the money handed over before he'd collected the gear. It was enough that an example needed making.

The house is cold when we get back. At the top of the stairs light bleeds beneath our mother's bedroom door.

- I'll say hello, Conor says.

- Leave her, it's late. She's probably fallen asleep reading. I tell him our sister will be over tomorrow, if she can get off work.

- Does she know why I'm here?

I nod. He seems indifferent to this. We hadn't involved her, other than my telling her I'd sort things, to not worry. Going to our brother wouldn't have been her approach, but families like ours don't go to the gardaí.

I search the cupboards. Mum's stash is significant but low on variety. I pour us each some cheap-looking vodka, ask Conor if he wants ice, but he just takes the glass from me.

I first heard of Davy Coughlan before moving away, a small-time loan shark operating out of the next estate. Neighbours sometimes used him in the run-up to Christmas, weekly repayments made on the doorstep, an informal yet binding arrangement. According to our sister, Coughlan's empire had grown as hard times returned, buying up the debts of several other illegal lenders, his reach spreading south down to Navan Road and beyond. He had several full-time collectors, men and women who squeezed what they could from you, latitude given if you promised to pay double the next week. And when you couldn't, someone more persuasive would call round, the tone shifting from community redeemer to something more menacing. Despite her alcoholism, our mother, as far as we knew, had always handled financial affairs ably, our father's absence focusing her mind on surviving alone with three children and a modest, unreliable income. And while we went without plenty, she managed to create the illusion that we weren't poor, fashioning free entertainment where possible, cheating the social out of a few quid. Since securing a half-decent job, I offered to send her money but it was always refused. Nobody knew for sure when she began using Coughlan, sometime after the last of us moved out, our sister thought.

- It was just enough to tide her over till her cheque came through, Sheenah had told me on the phone last week. Like getting stuff from the catalogue, paying it back here and there.

- How much?

- She'd never say, told me not to worry.

- So you didn't?

- I don't think you get to be critical anymore.

- But she was paying it off?

- She almost had, but Coughlan's goons convinced her to borrow more, to pay off the last of the first loan and have some leftover, and it carried on like this. I did a rough calculation of the interest rate, it's crazy. Last week someone came round, started asking who owned the house, took some jewellery as collateral.

- Why didn't she go to the bank?

- Don't be so naïve.

Conor pours us another drink, large ones. Despite the circumstances of our reunion, it's a relief to escape for now the path my own shortcomings are tempting me along. For the best part of a term I've ignored the unambiguous attentions of a pupil in my A-level class, dismissing the thoughts as they gather in my mind, telling myself such crushes were a vocational inevitability, that they pass with time. A promising cellist, the girl's compositional techniques were far advanced of her peers, and although I liked to encourage the creation of ensemble pieces, she excelled as a solo performer, the sublimity of her music the contrast of these shitty streets I grew up in. And for now I've behaved with utter professionalism, the line in my mind clear and precise, the problems with my relationship never allowed to dictate a gesture – behaviour barely noticed at first, yet the preamble to downfall. I imagine Conor faced with a similar situation, regarding its glorious potential, life holding such simplicity for his kind, the devoted servant of hedonism, of base needs.

My brother downs his drink. As his shirt rises I glimpse a heavily tattooed arm and remember the ones we gave each other as kids, crosses clumsily scrawled on our biceps, my own now weathered to an indistinct blue-green blemish. We pierced each other's ears too, a bloody affair, Conor's becoming infected, though he stuck with it, sporting to this day a silver ring. Other memories return unbidden. Of escaping the city's clutches, walking for miles, climbing trees to add to our collection of birds' eggs, a cache that presumably still lies in the loft here.

We started a fire once, in a barn we'd broken into, watching from a distant hill as the flames grew, feeling perhaps it had gone too far. Or just that it was something to regret, the wanton destruction of someone's property, an act other kids would have regarded frivolous, but that left us sombre for a day or two.

He asks about Mum, berates me for not visiting more.

- Work's busy just now.

- She needs looking after.

- Perhaps we should all come and live with you, play golf every day.

- With your fair skin? You'd last a week.

- I'll bring a hat.

I tell him more about Coughlan, stuff our sister had said.

- Right, he says, we do this tomorrow night.

- I've been thinking we should just pay it off. I've got some savings.

- You can wait in the car if you like. I'll go in on my own.

- You want me to come?

- Someone has to drive. Come on, you're good at that these days.

I want to say how absurd this all is, now that it's real. That I have a good job, more than that, I have a career to think of. There should be a more rational response to consider.

- Anyway, he says, why call me if you've doubts?

Because I knew you'd come back. Because I miss having you around. Because you just left, my younger yet somehow older brother.

- I don't know.

Conor tops us up once more.

- Your car reliable? he asks, and I nod. Good. Tomorrow, then. Best get some kip.

I gesture towards the spare room, offer to take the sofa.

- I'm fine on there, he says. You take the bed.

The next day we leave a few hours after dark. What sleep I'd managed was fitful, occupied by the formless spectres of fear, Conor's snoring a comfort on waking. Earlier our mother had cooked for the four of us, the food from another generation but surprisingly agreeable. She seemed unconcerned by my brother's sudden presence, delighting in the rare convergence of all her children. Our sister, too, imparted none of her usual animosity at our enduring absence.

After dinner Conor made some calls, presumably to get an address, perhaps to say hello to old friends. We'd searched the house and shed for something of Dad's, an old hurling stick or cricket bat, settling for a small crowbar from the garage. And then we go, across town, streets slicked with rain, lamps jaundicing the way. Conor's cigarette fills the car with a piquant fug, evoking some long forgotten aspect of our father, who would sit smoking for hours at the dining table, gazing at the window, perhaps planning his exodus.

My brother was disciplined, as our father termed it, most weeks, sometimes following a letter from school highlighting his absence or some misdemeanour. Or he'd come in late, dinner missed, clothes torn from a fight, his punishment rarely administered in the sobriety of the moment, reserved instead for a Friday night once the pub had closed, when the house was still and I'd listen to Conor's muffled cries through my bedroom wall.

Our father never struck me, though, as if my brother soaked up all his violent reserves. Around the time we set fire to the barn, I'd begun messing about in the garage, sitting in the Cortina listening to a tape, easing the gearstick back and forth, imagining some girl next to me, wind in her hair, the promise of lustful delights. One day, for reasons I can't recall, our father walked the two miles to work and on returning from school I found the car keys hanging in the hallway, figuring that a single lap of the garage block would go unnoticed. Unable to adjust the seat, I could barely reach the pedals, yet went ahead anyway, seduced by the engine's roar, by the drama of the thing.

The damage was minimal but impossible to miss, our father certain to discover it the following day. Later I showed Conor, who laughed an unconvincing laugh as we crouched together in the garage, inspecting the outcome of my misadventure.

- He loves this car, was all my brother said.

Dinner that evening was the usual quiet affair, Sheenah pushing vegetables from one side of her plate to the other, our mother lost to thoughts of some other life she might have led. I could hardly eat for fear, an image of the dented and scratched wing vivid in my mind. Out looking for nests once, Conor had spoken of the belt used, thick and ridged, its swift movement leaving the air behind it charged.

How many times? I'd asked, both wanting and not wanting to know. To get through it, Conor told me he imagined me standing behind our father, carrying out the same sentence on him, blow by blow.

When my brother spoke at dinner that night, it was almost with nonchalance, the act of lying coming easily to him by then, as he described how his foot had slipped on the pedal, how he tried to brake in time, the sound of metal on brick. How he would save his pocket money and pay for the repairs. Our father listened to the confession in silence, before heading out to the garage, where he stayed until it got dark.

As always the reckoning came days later, the whole house seeming to resound with the violence, our father going too far this time, even for him. And perhaps he feared he'd kill my brother one day, as the world seemed reordered after that night. Either way, he left a week later.

Conor asks about the car, what it does to the gallon. He seems relaxed, as if we're visiting family or heading for a night out, remarking on all the changes to this part of town.

- Ever thought of coming back? I say.

- Not really.

- Perhaps it's all been forgotten.

- These people don't forget. Anyway, come back for what?

- You could head my way. No one knows you there.

- Do you know how much rain southern Spain gets?

- Fair enough.

Conor flicks his cigarette out the window, tells me to take a left up ahead.

- You all settled down with Jane now? he says.

- I guess.

- Don't it scare you, the same woman for the rest of your life?

- Why should it?

- No variety, never fucking someone for the first time again.

- There's more than fucking.

He laughs, as if I couldn't possibly believe this, and for a moment, after all these years, I almost ask him why he did it. Instead I say, Do you ever wonder where he went? What he's doing?

- No, not really.

I wait in the car, apparently to keep watch but effectively redundant, a provider of transport, hands and conscience clean, eyes witness to nothing more than the initial orchestration. I wonder how often my brother does something like this these days, whether there are others in his adopted country who take care of such matters for him now.

- Some people only understand one way, one language, he'd said last night.

- And if it makes things worse for her?

- I'll come back.

A young couple, a little drunk, sidle along the pavement, the man stumbling into the wing mirror, knocking it askew, the woman apologising before laughing. I try to hunker down, feign indifference, but the man – a boy really, I see now – feels the need to make a point, his face an inch from the windscreen, breath misting the glass as he studies me. You need to go, I want to say. You need to go before my brother returns and events go badly for you. The girl pulls his coat, pleads with him, a hint in her voice of being witness to such events too often. My giving him nothing to feed off eventually works and after a final flourish of menace he allows the girl to lead him away, down the road, the boy howling into the night like some demented creature.

I stare at the building across the road, the door Conor entered, trying to calculate how long it's been, how many men Coughlan might have up there. I'd made him promise just to issue a warning, his visit a symbol of our resistance, that we, that our mother, wouldn't simply roll over and pay up.

It occurs to me that we should have parked further away, that bringing the car here in an age of ubiquitous CCTV was foolish. I consider how frightened by everything I am – being here now, the aggression of a passing boy, the guilt of an imagined affair – all of it taking me back to the dinner table that night, to the disciplining Conor saved me from.

Had I always been a coward? So innately weak that even our father was reluctant to expose it, made as I am of different stuff? Perhaps Conor is on some level thankful for the man's brutish hand, it hardening him, forging him like a blacksmith's hammer, preparing him for the world he would know.

Stepping out of the car I can smell my childhood, a thousand memories assembling at the promise of their indulgence. I picture Jane reading in our bed, my safe and comfortable life so removed from this place, yet the link never entirely severed. I imagine my class on Monday, the ruinous thoughts that will line up in attack formation. How I'll do the right thing and be resentful for it. I consider my sister's face, how something in her eyes resembles utterly my own, our complexions alike – ashen, almost ethereal – Conor's swarthy by comparison, even before his expatriation, marking him out for our father's attention from the start.

Unsolicited, a mealtime routine of sorts comes to mind, a rare glimpse of another side to our father, who whenever my brother asked if he could get down from the table, would reply, No, son, you can only get down from a duck. He said it in response without fail, the two of them trading guarded smiles as if it was the first time.

Perhaps I will go to visit, get away from it all for a while, arrive with every flavour of crisp. Jane might come, the trip a new start, the sun nourishing us. I picture finding Conor on the tee, his grip loosened a little as the club scythes downward, connecting cleanly, the ball cutting without deviation through crystalline Spanish sky, mile after mile.

The city is quieter now, burnished in moonlight. Ignoring my heart's frequent, heavy beat, I open the door across the street, negotiate the stairs in near-darkness, almost tripping as I run to find my brother.

Jennifer Allott

Jennifer Allott was born and brought up in York. She lives in Chesham, Buckinghamshire with her husband and two sons and works as a manager in local government. *Mid-air* is her first published work.

Mid-air

Alex managed not to puke until they were past Pickering. Puke was a good word. It was properly like the thing. The sudden heave and then the GURLCH as it all shot out. Alex's puke was pink from the bubble gum flavoured ice cream he had eaten in Robin Hood's Bay.

Alex had realised what was going to happen, had recognised that strange cold crawly feeling and said, "Dad ... please!"

Dad had said, "God, I thought you'd grown out of it. Shit"

"Dad, quickly!"

"Alex I can't stop here!"

"I'm going to ..."

"Get out! Get out!"

He leapt out from the back seat of dad's Sierra and as the puke came flying out he realised Paula had opened her door too. She hadn't understood Alex bellowing from the back seat and dad desperately checking the mirrors and screeching on to the verge. And so GURLCH she had a splash of bubble gum flavour ice cream puke all over her shoe and up her leg.

It had not been a good day. In fact, thought Alex, wiping his mouth on the back of his hand, it had been a really bad day. He climbed back in the car and slammed the door hard. He saw dad's shoulders hunch but dad couldn't say anything anymore. He just has to live with it, thought Alex, with satisfaction.

"Robin Hood's Bay is my favourite place in the world," dad had said to
Paula as they set off from York that morning. "I've been going there since
I was a boy."

"It was mum's favourite place too," said Alex. "But I doubt it is any
more."

There was silence for the rest of the journey. Alex looked out of the
window and Rosie slept. Rosie did not understand who Paula was. She was
three, but when she slept she still looked like a baby. Her cheeks flushed
a deep pink and curls lifted off her forehead in the breeze from the open
window. Alex took hold of Rosie's hand. She didn't stir.

Alex had been trying to be nice to people, and that included Rosie.
Being nice to people was not hard, but you had to keep an eye on it. At
school Alex was being nice to the new boy Ben. To begin with this was
hard as Ben had a large head and a squint and talked about bus routes a lot.
But with practice Alex found he quite liked Ben. Ben knew lots of facts.
He particularly knew facts about disasters. And if you concentrated on this
and not on Ben's strange head, liking him was really quite easy.

"Did you know," said Ben, "that a man once drove a bus across Tower
Bridge in London when it was open?"

Alex didn't know that Tower Bridge opened, or where it was, so Ben
explained.

"The man was called Albert Gunther and when he drove on to the bridge
with twenty people in his bus the bridge started lifting and he thought,
'Oh shit'."

This was a good thing about Ben. He swore and it was just normal. He
didn't seem to think it was naughty or anything.

"So he had to decide whether to slam on the brakes or what. And he just accelerated and the bus flew through the air, over the gap and bang! Down on the other side. The bus was a number 78."

When mum had told Alex and Rosie that dad was not coming back, Alex did not really know what happened. BANG. She just told them. They were watching Crystal Maze in the lounge and mum had come in and sat in a chair watching them and not looking at the telly. She just sat on the settee and watched for a long time and Alex had reached out and taken Rosie's hand.

"To the Crystal Dome!" shouted the man on telly, and Alex fixed his eyes on the screen. He wondered if they could just sit like this for ever. If mum didn't say it, then dad would come back. The contestants crossed the drawbridge and it was pulled up, just like Tower Bridge.

"Will you start the fans please!" the man shouted.

Alex couldn't remember what mum said exactly, but he could remember mum trying to pick Rosie off the carpet and then him running upstairs and hiding in his bed. Mum had come up with Rosie, who was sucking her thumb and they both sat on the end of his bed. He wiped his nose and eyes on his pillow and nobody told him off.

"It'll be alright Alex," said mum.

But it wasn't.

When they arrived at Robin Hood's Bay that morning they had parked at the top of the cliff. Rosie would not hold anyone's hand but Alex's as they walked the narrow cobbled streets. They were slow because of all the steps. Dad and Paula would disappear round the corner and Alex and Rosie would follow after like a four-legged creature.

"We're a great sea monster with two heads and four legs!" said Alex, hugging Rosie. She smelt of cornflakes.

"RAAAH!" said Rosie and they both laughed.

They had lunch in a café in a street perched high on the cliff. The houses all leaned against each other like wobbly teeth. They carried their trays to a table on a terrace at the back and Paula put her sunglasses on. A fly landed on Alex's chips.

"Isn't this lovely?" said dad.

"Heaven," said Paula and took his hand.

Ben had told Alex that flies eat by puking on their food which turns the food to mush and they suck it up with a long stalk which they have instead of a mouth. Alex looked at the fly carefully. If he looked at the fly he didn't have to look at dad holding Paula's hand. The fly walked all the way along the chip but he couldn't see any puke.

"I don't like chips," said Rosie.

"Just eat the sausage then," said dad.

"Did you know that flies have to puke on their food before they eat it?" said Alex.

"Alex!" said dad.

"I need a wee-wee," said Rosie.

"Oh, Rosie," said dad.

When Rosie got down from the chair Alex could see a dark patch blooming on the front of her shorts.

"It's too late dad", he said.

"You're too old for this," said dad, and Rosie let out a long wail, leaning forward so no one could see the patch.

"She's only been doing it since you left," said Alex, looking up from the fly.

There was nothing dad could say to that, thought Alex grimly, and he watched as Paula looked at dad.

"We haven't got spare clothes," said Alex.

"Don't worry," said Paula, "I've got a t-shirt back at the car. You come with me sweetie and we'll get you sorted out."

Rosie threw herself forward onto the ground. Alex ate a chip and listened to the wails. Paula and dad knelt by Rosie and said sorry to the couple at the other table on the terrace. Dad carried Rosie out through the café.

"Did you know," said Alex, as Paula sat down opposite him and they both carried on with their lunch, "that in 1954 a man drove across Tower Bridge when it was opening in a bus with twenty passengers."

"No, I didn't know that," said Paula. "Were they all OK?"

"They were fine," said Alex. "What do you think they thought when the bus went hurtling through the air?"

"Oooh!" said Paula, as if this was a really good question. "Maybe they were excited. Maybe they thought they would fly to the moon!"

"I think they all thought they were going to die," said Alex.

They ate on in silence until dad and Rosie came back. Rosie was wearing a very big Global Hypercolor t-shirt that must belong to Paula.

"You've got a Global Hypercolor t-shirt!" said Alex to Paula before he could stop himself. Paula smiled and Alex thought about mum and what she was doing at home.

Alex wondered what it was about mum that dad didn't like anymore. When the weather was hot mum's ankles got all puffy and she put them up on the pouf in the sitting room. They weren't very nice to look at. But that was not enough to leave. Really dad should try being nice like Alex tried, and try to think about the good things about mum and not about the bad things like her puffy ankles.

Alex leant over to where Rosie was curled in dad's lap and put his hand on her back. The t-shirt slowly turned from pink to purple from the heat of his hand. He could feel Rosie's back hiccupping from all the crying.

"This is Paula from work," said dad, when Alex and Rosie had first met her, the week before.

They were on the swings in the park, and it seemed that Paula just happened to be out for a jog at the very same time. Alex looked at Paula. As he swung down he saw her long curly hair tied up in a scrunchy, then her shocking pink lycra t-shirt then her hands with red-painted nails holding her Walkman, then thin brown ankles and big white trainers. Up and down. Trainers, ankles, Walkman, nails, t-shirt, hair, t-shirt, nails, Walkman, ankles, trainers.

"Say hello to Paula, Alex," said dad.

"Hello," said Alex, swinging higher.

Before she left, Paula had planted a big kiss on Rosie's cheeks. Rosie picked up the bottom of her pinafore and wiped her face.

"Bye Alex, bye Rosie," Paula had said and she put her earphones back on her head and jogged away.

The afternoon was hot. They sat on the beach. Paula listened to her Walkman and dad stretched out on the sand next to her. Alex and Rosie went to look at the rock pools. The first one they came to was small and the surface was smooth. Alex lay down and looked into the slimy green water. He blew on the pool and watched the ripple expand. An insect landed on the surface of the pool and walked across it. Alex gasped. He would have to tell Ben. Each tiny leg rested on the surface of the pool. Alex blew again, the insect stopped and then, after the water had calmed, started to walk again. Alex put his hand in the water and churned it round, moving closer to the insect. He watched as it was dragged beneath the surface of the pool and disappeared into the grimy water. When Alex walked back along the beach to dad and Paula, Rosie was not there.

"Where's Rosie?" asked dad.

Alex stared. The next ten minutes there was a funny feeling in the bottom of Alex's stomach. Dad ran along the beach down by the shore and Paula headed off towards the road.

"Come on Alex," she shouted. They ran along shouting Rosie's name. Alex noticed a small sandy path winding up the cliff. He ran up it. As the path reached the top of the cliff he could suddenly see across fields towards a row of grey hills. Rosie was sitting in the long grass.

"Hiya Alex," she said.

When they walked down the path, Paula held Rosie's hand, and Rosie didn't mind.

"Do you guys want an ice cream?" asked Paula after they'd found dad. There were so many flavours to choose from that Alex couldn't make up his mind.

"Which would you have?" he asked dad, but dad was busy talking to Rosie, so Paula answered.

"Bubble gum."

They continued their drive home in silence. Alex leaned his forehead against the cold glass of the window and watched the boring flat bit before York arrived. The road slid on straight ahead and it began to rain. Nobody was talking and Alex could see Paula trying to wipe the sick off her shoe with a tissue. It had been a bad day. It was hard to be nice to people all the time when they weren't always nice to you. But that didn't mean you should stop trying.

"I think maybe," said Alex, considering each word carefully before it came out, "that me and Rosie are getting poorly. Rosie wet herself and cried a lot and I was sick, so I think we are probably getting poorly."

Alex saw Paula and dad look at each other. He turned back to the rainy window. As the drops rolled past Alex's eyes he thought about the number 78 bus.

"Can you imagine what it must have been like?" Ben had asked Alex. "Can you imagine one minute being on the road and then the road is gone and you're hurtling through space?"

At the time Alex said he couldn't imagine. He'd thought about the passengers quite a bit since then, sitting on the bus heading to the shops or to their work, and then suddenly realising that the ground had dropped away and they were in mid-air. He'd thought about it, and he'd begun to think that actually he could imagine, he could imagine what that was like.

Martyn Bryant

Martyn Bryant is from Windsor. He holds two masters degrees, an MSc in Physics from the University of British Columbia, Canada, which he received in 2007, and an MA in Creative Writing from Birkbeck University in London, which he received this year. Since completing the MA he has moved to Montreal, Canada and has had short stories published in *Feathertale, RYGA, The Mechanics' Institute Review 11*, and forthcoming in *Carte Blanche*. In addition to writing short stories Martyn is working on his first novel, which was partly developed in May at The Banff Centre four-week Writing Studio. http://martynbryant.wordpress.com/

Album Review:
Thoughts of Home by
We Thought We Were Soldiers

Until the mid-2000s we had been lost and lonely. Lennon was dead. Buckley was dead. Churchill was dead. Jesus was dead. Nobody alive was making good music. We didn't have boyfriends and girlfriends and we lived with our parents and slept in single beds in towns whose hopes and dreams had been reduced to waiting for a new 24-hour Tesco to open. We all wondered whether university had been worth it. Perhaps, as promised in the prospectus, it gave us the 'teamworking' skills to continue to work full-time at HMV even though the other employees were incompetent, and the 'self-motivation' skills to continue for two years writing reviews of unremarkable bands on London music blogs that nobody read.

That was until we heard We Thought We Were Soldiers.

In just 28 minutes that night, they spoke a truth we had never heard before. In just 28 minutes they demonstrated that Plato was wrong; there was a perfect version of music in the real world and they created it. In a pub. In Hoxton. In just 28 minutes they also taught us to how to fly.

After the gig, like always, we were too embarrassed to stay and talk to strangers so we walked north towards the canal and tried flying and it worked. Flying was actually a piece of piss. We flew over Regent's Canal and The Angel and landed at our national rail terminals on the other side of the ticket barriers to save us the fares. We took trains to our 24h-Tesco-waiting towns and then flew over the ticket barriers again and continued home. We blogged at 2:23 am and 14 minutes later we got comments like, "Yes, they were holy fuck. Will you be there again tomorrow? I'll be dressed in red and white like the Canadian flag." They were the first comments in two years that weren't from our brothers saying, "Wanker," or our sisters saying, "Who reads this? I fucking don't."

By breakfast over thirty people had read the post and we were ready to dream again.

We returned to the Hoxton pub the following evening and danced with boys and girls dressed in red and white and we tried not to spill our pints. WTWWS played for another 28 minutes and this time we listened more intently. They were influenced by everything in the known world and nothing in the known world; it was less musical and more musical than anything we'd heard before.

Their music taught us to be confident enough not to leave straight after the gig. We stayed for another pint and waited in line for a self-titled demo, standing awkwardly next to Canadians, discussing if and how we should classify WTWWS. We thought of vague genres like 'nova-resurgence' and 'new-indie', neither of which did them justice. We coined the term 'post-music' and everyone else in the queue agreed it was apt.

We flew with the Canadian girls and boys back to their King's College residences and as we listened to the demo's seven tracks, in stark rooms with just a bed and a sink, we learnt to become post-virginal. We had arrived in a new age.

In the morning we flew with sex hair from the dorms, over Admiral Nelson, and onto our London terminals. We landed in front of Delice de France counters for ham-cheese croissants before flying over the ticket barriers and taking 8am trains to our 24h-Tesco-waiting towns. WTWWS had arrived and they'd made us adults.

Still Animals

We had to wait for a year for the first record and it was as good as the demo, numinous post-music with post-poetic lyrics. If the first record taught us how to love and showed us how to get beautiful Canadian boyfriends and girlfriends, the second album taught us patience - lots of monogamous-post-virginal-patience while we tried to save enough money to get to Canada and rejoin our lovers.

We skyped our boyfriends and girlfriends and told them that we found it easy to remain monogamous and then we fell asleep thinking of them fucking other people. WTWWS taught us how to cope with jealousy, they taught us to cope with jealousy really well.

They played the *Still Animals* material live in Alexandra Palace. We were alone and embarrassed to be alone. We stood closer than necessary to girls and boys who wore opium perfume/cologne. It didn't matter. Ally Pally was packed. WTWWS were so good that afterwards we flew over Hampstead Heath and onto our national rail terminals.

We flew into the stations with only 2 minutes before the last trains were to leave. It was too late to wait for burgers to be cooked so we took whatever was ready, onion rings, and we had to eat them on the trains. Embarrassed by the smell we ate them as quickly as possible and then wiped our oily hands on the fabric seats.

Arriving home, we wrote reviews, slept, woke, edited and filed them with our editors at national magazines and newspapers before we went to our HMVs and tried to convince the managers that the hip-hop section needed to be renamed the self-help section.

Thoughts of Home

And now, two years after *Still Animals*, three years after the self-titled demo, We Thought We Were Soldiers release their new record *Thoughts of Home*. Our expectations couldn't have been higher. Where would post-music go next? Would they leave post-music behind and develop a new unimaginable genre?

Not quite.

In terms of progression, the record starts off cautiously. That said, it is still blissfully rooted within the post-music tradition. Track 1 is like the pleasure of waking up in a bed that our Canadian girlfriends and boyfriends have vacated a few hours earlier. We can stretch fully and to our relief our backs don't have a dull nagging pain.

Track 2 ends with a short sequence that hints that WTWWS are continuing to evolve as a band. The relief of hearing this progression is like the relief we experienced 4 months ago when we got back into Canada.

We had been in Canadian International airports and wrote on the customs forms that we wanted entry as tourists for the maximum 6 months – we'd been in Canada for the previous 6 months as tourists also, with just a week in the UK in between. The buzz-cut border guards didn't believe that we could make enough money by working remotely as music journalists for UK newspapers and magazines. In truth, we couldn't. They also thought that we were trying to reside in Canada as tourists. We weren't, but we kind of were. They went behind one-way glass and phoned our boyfriends and girlfriends to make sure that we weren't working illegally. As we waited we imagined being forced to purchase tickets for the next flights back to London. Somehow our girlfriends and boyfriends said the right thing and we were released into the arrivals areas where we shook with relief as we kissed them. We were almost too shaken up to fly to their apartments but we managed somehow by holding hands.

Track 3 teaches us that we need to communicate more so we telephone our mothers and when they say towards the end, "I think that's all the news I've got for now," it reminds them that, "Oh, the new 24h Tesco is now open but only until midnight each day. The locals can't buy hot cross buns at two in the morning." There's love in the 2nd track too, the kind of love that makes us say, "Love you loads Mum."

Track 4 makes us want to communicate better with the world. We message our Canadian lovers to say, "I look forward to seeing you tonight, I hope you're having a good day at work."
    The last 20 seconds of this track are quite interesting, the song comes across as a little parable that says to us that we need regular exercise to help maximise happiness.

Track 5 plunges our heads under water. After swimming 35 lengths of front crawl using our undergrad learnt 'self-motivation' we get out and shower ourselves next to men and women who spend their whole shower-time scrubbing their genitals.

And then begins the slide away from their post-music roots. Track 6 is a poor imitation of what they've done before. Our respective girlfriends and boyfriends message us back, "I'll be home late tonight, too much work." We get the sense that they are staying at work late to spite us.

We thought WTWWS always had a nuanced approach to melancholia but in track 7 they lose that nuance and the music is trying to rationalise its way out of paranoia, like the paranoia that our lovers aren't coming home from work anytime soon. It's as if we were to message, using the best of our 'teamworking' skills that we'd learnt in undergrad, "Good luck!"

Track 8 is surprising, it's like receiving a message that says, "I'm going out with Sarah for a drink," and we message with more of our 'teamworking' skills, "oh, ok, I'll keep working my way through We Thought We Were Soldiers' new record. I don't like it."

Track 9 is all re-hashed parts of the demo, which taught us to fly, and parts of Still Animals, which taught us to be patient.

Track 10 is more of the same, more of the same waiting, being patient and hopeful to hear something ending on a high with messages that say, "Home in a min, x", but really they say, "Don't wait up, I'm staying for a second drink."

Our 'teamworking' skills aren't really sure how to shape the next messages. We consider, "Ok, I'm glad you're having fun," but we don't send anything. Track 10 is the longest track on the record by far.

Listening to track 11 makes it difficult to sleep, it makes us wonder what's wrong and what our online dating profiles will sound like: "30 years old, music reviewer, looking for someone to help me find a genre of music that can't be categorised as self-help."

Track 12 is like the devastation of laying in a bed in silence with our girlfriends and boyfriends sleeping beside us, knowing that they'll never kiss us again. Under those circumstances it is impossible to sleep.

Overall, with *Thoughts of Home,* We Thought We Were Soldiers have become a pathetic and jaded self-parody. They sound like the wannabe post-music bands that are trying to imitate them. Their lyrics have also gone from transcendent post-poetic to incoherent proto-poetic. We used to think we were soldiers, but really we were just deluded. They had been leading us somewhere else, somewhere better, but they stopped, they let go of our hands and started doing distracting things like making babies, etc.

In some ways the album is subtly saying that we need to take individual responsibility for our actions. In that vein:

I am learning that Plato was right and there is no such thing as perfection in music or girlfriends. I now need to learn how to fall asleep even though everything is fucked up. However, I need the toilet. On the way to the bathroom I look out of the window. Under the street light, Lennon, Buckley, Churchill and Jesus are flying. Churchill is surprisingly good at flying for a fatty.

Post-music is dead.

Rating 3.4/10

Chris Edwards-Pritchard

Chris Edwards-Pritchard currently works in the fundraising team of a world-leading conservation charity, and scribbles short stories in his spare time. He graduated from Royal Holloway University in 2011 with a BA in English and Creative Writing and wrote several still-birth novels before focusing on short stories. He has been shortlisted for the Gregory Maguire Award as well as the Bristol Short Story Prize. Chris admires the work of Vonnegut, Saunders and Chabon, and hopes to one day write with half as much beauty and charisma as those three magicians.

Terrorism and Tourism

It's my first day as Hostage 17. Amita Choudrey, The Red Widow, stands in front of me with a tangle of wires and batteries and pretend explosives strapped underneath her niqab, and a semi-automatic by her side. The crowd of visitors are silent. We hope they are crapping, have crapped, or are preparing to crap their pants. A few have already surrendered their £40 admission; hobbling out of Exit Door G. The Red Widow shoots me, but I forget to activate the Blood Pack. I fall counter-trajectory toward the visitors into the lap of a Japanese grandpa who thinks this is the funniest thing in the world. He invites his whole extended family to take photos of him laughing and pointing at the fake dead english man inches away from his. Which will no doubt become the crowning jewel of their London photo album. I hold my breath and am on the verge of actually dying when The Red Widow goes Off Script dragging me out of the Jap's lap. And saying: put the phones and cameras away or you're next you little kuffar dickweeds.

I've been at Holden Tower: The Live Terrorism Experience for eight months. Only just promoted from Lift Attendant in Zone 2 where I got to tackle Ginge Gleeson to the ground every forty minutes of the day. Rotations are forty minutes apart. He played Lift Panicker, a claustrophobic burger flipping Minnesotan on a tour of the UK. I tackled him and every time he said: what the hella you doin', this ain't American football buddy. Which was easily one of the worst lines in the Script.

Sally-Ann was happy that I got the promotion. It was just about the only thing that had made her happy since my mother broke her leg the day before our wedding. When I first got the Lift Attendant job Sally-Ann was really pissed because I'd taken a pay cut from my role as Bogtrotter on the Planet Stealers UK tour. But this time she was all smiles even though the rise was pittance. I said I can't understand you, and she was like: Daniel, I'm pregnant again.

Dammit-.

The Red Widow and I, Hostage 17, were both cautioned for going Off Script. Peter Hoskins, the MD, calls us into his office just moments after the final Rotation of the day as visitors are cathartically pouring into the Gift Shop to claim their 'I Survived Holden Tower' memorabilia and gawp at their Official Photographs, which are always a right hoot but hardly sell. Hoskins is a small guy with a wiry moustache. The Red Widow whose real name is Elena Balchov takes a seat opposite Hoskins without removing her Zone 4 costume: suicide corset and half-torn niqab. This makes him click his pen. Elena, he says, my dear this is kind of the fourth time you've gone Off Script this month. I jump in and say I'm really sorry but this is completely my fault. Hoskins says: we kind of paid Paul Webster a lot of money to write the Script so please stay within the Improvisation Guidelines, which advise against inaccurate colloquialisms such as dickweed and what have you. Elena makes a sound. Somewhere in between a cough and a yawn and a grunt. It's not inaccurate, she says with the niqab still concealing her face. Unlike your writer, she continues, I've met with Choudrey's old school teachers, ex-bosses, second cousins and found that her all time favourite insult was: dickweed. Hoskins nods and closes his eyes and wishes us both a lovely evening.

We walk back down to Costume. Thanks for sticking up for me in there, she says slipping the niqab off over her head and unclipping the vest. I couldn't tell whether she was joking or not. She was The Red Widow and I was just Lift Attendant now Hostage 17 and I hadn't really had a conversation with her before or indeed seen her in non-costume attire. So when that dusty niqab came off you can just imagine the slight rise of my eyebrows and the sudden awareness of my every footstep and my desperately trying not to gaze at her for too long but wanting to gaze at her forever until that brown frizz and slanted smirk were burnt onto my retina and. I mean it, she says, thanks for telling him it was your fault. I smile because that's the only thing I can do. She adds: because it was your fault. And then winks. And then walks in front so I get to witness the full beauty of that plump-.

That night after I've tucked Mavis into bed and pinky promised her that the wardrobe is for clothes not grandad's neighbours (Bermondsey meth addicts) I pour a glass of red and ask Sally-Ann about her day. She speaks her reply at the television. Programme about boat renovations. And I watch the television whilst she speaks her reply. Wife: something about cake, something about the park, something about a rotten salesman, something about something. Great, I say, that sounds real great honey. A guy on the television buys a shoddy canal boat and makes a joke about being in deep water. We both laugh. Then Sally-Ann says would you mind grabbing me those tortilla chips we opened on Saturday? I say no of course not, but in my head I'm like are you sure what about an apple for once what about all those dresses you chucked away last week pregnancy isn't an excuse for obesity you know. I go to the kitchen and I sulk. She didn't even ask me about my first day as Hostage 17. But that's nothing new. So long as it pays the bills. She tolerates my acting in inverted commas so long as my acting in inverted commas pays the bills. So I've got by with paid summer work in the Horror Maze at Regent's Park as a limping zombie, and picked up the odd seasonal role here and there; an elf, a ghoul, a bunny rabbit. I've made ends meet. The stage is where I really want to be. But Holden Tower: The Live Terrorism Experience is as good a stage as any: an anti-Brechtian promenade theatre at the cutting edge of modern historical re-enactment. That's what our Corporate Brochure says. Who needs applause anyway. I grab the tortilla chips that we opened on Saturday.

The next morning in the Staff Area I get chatting to Sammy Levine, a bulky sour lad who went to St Christophers in Lewisham with Sally-Ann and her brothers. They still meet up for a pint every now and then. He works in IT but always tells anybody who will listen that IT should be split into two departments: Surveillance and Technical, because Surveillance has been taking up a big chunk of his time ever since Hoskins got the mid-year data on non-paying admissions. I saw you and Elena went Off Script yesterday, says Sammy. You did, I say, what a monumental cock-up, eh? He shakes his head and tells me: Hoskins would never have known if he wasn't in Surveillance breathing down my neck at the time it happened. He adds: this isn't what I signed up for.

I have an apple and go straight through to Costume. Most of Zones 1 and 2 are in there in a long line of chairs and mirrors having their hair and make-up done. Ginge Gleeson is by the Exit Door to Zone 1 hoiking his fake beer belly up a little so it doesn't chafe. We high five and he says: this ain't American football buddy, which gets a big laugh.

Elena is always the last to show up in Zone 3, the open plan office. Sometimes she enters just seconds before the elevator doors ping open to reveal a cluster of tentative visitors. This creates a palpable pre-show tension. On cue: Exit Door G swings open and in comes Elena dressed in that blue niqab and showing off her semi-automatic as if it were a water hose. She sweeps from one end of the office to the other and when the elevator pings she charges at the visitors and they compress to the back of the lift with quivering legs and arms shielding heads and mothers clutching children. The Red Widow: put your useless kuffar hands above your heads and get in here now or in the name of Allah I will blow your brains to Bracknell and back. All in the Script. She shoves some of them. She's allowed to do that. There are various signs that say: you may be touched by the Actors but not harmed. If at any time you feel uncomfortable please say Get Me Out and an Actor will direct you to the nearest Exit Door. She calls them pieces of shit and smacks Hostage 13, young Jez Hope, round the face when he attempts to alert the police. What a woman. Such a physical command of the space. Before I even know it she's pulling me in front of the visitors and pointing the butt of the semi at my heart and yelling about the God that loves her and the paradise that awaits her. Superb delivery, such timing. At this point, I, and by that I mean Hostage 17, should really be crapping his pants and thinking of his family, of young made-up Jarvis and the other kid who's still a bun in the estranged wife's oven and maybe even thinking of the estranged wife herself despite her estrangement. But instead the mind of Hostage 17 is brimming with Elena Amita who is a right turn-on with or without the damn niqab and if he, Hostage 17, is to perish then what better way to go: the bullet of a beautiful woman striking his heart and him falling backwards slow-motionally with a smile on his face as his hand presses the trouser pocket button to release the Blood Pack, which is nothing more than a happy, happy ejaculation.

And then: hits his actual head on side of desk.

Dammit.

A gasp. At the back of the group of visitors an old lady with a face like an ice field yells: Get me out! And so sacrifices her £40 admission.

Once the visitors have been herded into Zone 4 the resurrected Hostages tell me that I should get my head checked out because it's actually bleeding and looks quite deep. But I'm like: we haven't got time before the next Rotation - and anyway, it adds to the look. I make it through to lunch and feel fine. It's six Rotations before lunch, and five after. And anyway: every time she shoots me I feel re-energised, as if she's doing the exact opposite of killing me. Such a buzz. Do it again, do it again. I don't even ring Sally-Ann at lunch for fear that she'll drag me out of this most wonderful state of mind with tales of visiting grandma and baking cookies and hunting for headlice. I don't even check the phone for messages. I'll tell her that we had a company-wide meeting. Script Revision, or somesuch.

At lunch I sit with Eber Petrelli who plays Raymond G. Skala the star of Zone 4 and the only survivor of the Holden Tower terror attack, who jumped from Floor 13 into a pond and survived to tell the tale. Eber is easily the nicest guy on set. A broad, welcoming face and the kind of slicked back grey hair that is only worn by senior gentlemen who are particularly at ease with the world, having made all the mistakes there are to make. This is a great place to re-learn everything that I unlearnt in Hollywood, he tells me as we dig into our limp baked potatoes in yellow plastic tubs. Note: complain to Catering on a moodier day. Eber points to the ceiling and says: here we get back to the very raw bones of acting. Won't be long before you're up in Zone 4. Remember, there are no small parts, Daniel, only small actors.

I ask him if he could say that last bit again so I can record it and have it as my ringtone. He laughs and bops me on the shoulder. What a nice guy. What a great day. I almost skip through the Canteen and think to myself that this is one of the best days of my career, if not my life. It's the kind of thought that turns my stomach over. I can't even remember how I felt when I first held Mavis? The bell goes for the first Rotation of the afternoon and I make my way through to Zone 3.

I'm ready to play. Elena pulls me to the centre of the office and she kills me a handful of times and I fall without hitting my head but making sure I land so as to show off the actual cut just above my brow. Somewhere in there I decide to mix it up a little and really struggle when she grabs me so that she has to resort to kicking me and yanking me by the fringe. It gets rough. Over the course of the afternoon no less than eight visitors yell: Get me out! which means we're really nailing the semiotics.

By the final Rotation I'm feeling a little woozy and the cut is bleeding again. Sally-Ann's going to be asking all kinds of questions when I get home and telling me that I'm an idiot for carrying on with a head wound. And then it will be all Angry Wife: this is the problem with your line of work Daniel if you get injured then we can't feed our daughter. I'm like: I've got it covered. Health insurance and so on. And then she does the thing where she fights back the tears in front of Mavis and hugs her for a little too long and tells her to shoosh when she isn't even saying a word. It's a real kick in the teeth.

Talking of which-.

Here's comes Elenas boot, just about missing my cheekbone.

This time I stand and run at her and all the other Hostages say what in the name of sweet Jesus are you doing, which is kind of Off Script but within their Improvisation Guidelines. Elena shoots me as I'm running and I willingly tumble to the ground squirting the Blood Pack onto some of the front row visitors, of which at least ninety percent crap their pants. I perform the blink-blink-blink-dead procedure with ease but just want to yell at Elena to do it again, and I can feel that she wants to do it again too, pausing a second too long standing over my corpse before yelling at the visitors to get on their feet, hands where she can see them and herding them through to Zone 4 where old Eber Petrelli is preparing to jump out of the window.

I'm in First Aid until well gone 7. Pretty much everyone has gone home and I still haven't checked my phone. I predict twenty missed calls and six messages. Jeez. The nurse wraps a bandage around my brow and advises me not to drive home and says I should share a cab with Elena Balchov who always gets a cab back to Camden around now. I find Elena alone in the Staff Room. She says: you're still here? I say: you still here? Her Zone 4 niqab is off, but she's wearing the suicide corset, as you do. Reading a magazine. Her hair is in a bun. She jangles a ring of keys. Come with me, she says, and I oblige. She walks in front of me down the corridor past Costume but she might as well be walking behind me with that gun honed at the small of my back. We end up in History of Terror Part Three a soundproof mini cinema which is the final holding pen before visitors enter Zone 1. It's empty. She locks the door and shoves me to the floor. The projector whirs and the speakers crackle. It's a short film about the Holden Tower attack narrated by James McLaughlin who has the voice of an out-of-tune glockenspiel. He says: there is no specific evidence to suggest why the Holden Tower was targeted, it was a seemingly ra-andom choice; a central London office block filled with unassuming and innocent human beings. Infiltration was simple and quick. A ha-andful of hostages were killed by gunfire, but the majority perished when Amita Choudrey, The Red Widow, detonated a device strapped to her waist and brought the building to the grou-und, killing three hundred and seventeen. [The projector spits out images of the tower falling at an angle, cloud of dust, running, flames, streams of blue flashing lights etc.] One man, Raymond G. Skala, jumped from the thirteenth floor into a pond and survived. Most of what you will experience is based on his eyewitness acco-unt. You are now about to enter Elena Balchov. Which isn't quite what he said, but no time for accuracy. I slide her knickers down. She unzips my jeans. It's scrappy, abrasive. She keeps the suicide belt on for a long as possible and only lets me unclip it when I'm inside her.

Dammit-.

I go straight to ASDAs and search for a nice bunch of flowers but then decide against the flowers because none of them are reduced and the thing with flowers is you might as well purchase a massive neon sign which flashes: I'm a cheating bastard. I buy a toy for Mavis instead, and some gum. My head pounds. As I pull up on the drive I see them both peering out the front window with the curtain draped over their heads as if they were wearing bloody burkas. That gives me the first heart attack of the night. I can't make out any facial expressions but I hope Sally-Ann is furious that I haven't answered my phone all day and come home late and maybe something happened during the day like Mavis being sick which was an absolute nightmare on it's own and only exacerbated by my not answering the phone and coming home late. I need her to be angry. But inside there's only concern. My baby what's happened oh my god your head are you okay were you attacked come here and sit down have you been to A and E come here don't ever do this to me again. Mavis hugs my leg as if she plans on never letting go. Sally-Ann: do you want paracetamol I was so worried I rang your work but nobody answered so I rang Sammy and he said you'd fallen and last thing he knew you were getting a taxi with Elaine-. Cue: second heart attack of the night. I'm like: you rang Sammy? Yeah I rang Sammy I was so worried I don't even care that you drove home I'm just glad you're here, home.

We have dinner. We play with Mavis. She's just about getting used to the idea of aeroplanes and thumping round the house with her arms spread to the side, ducking and diving. Neenaw, she says. And I say no Mavis neenaw is an ambulance, whoosh is an aeroplane. Whishh, she says.

When Elena kills me the next morning it's quick and clinical and takes everybody by surprise including myself, with Blood Pack erupting a second too late. And then quick as a flash she's herding the visitors onwards to Zone 4; all a bit dazed and confused it being only half past nine on a drizzly Thursday morning. The doors hiss shut. Blimey, says Hostage 12, she's a bit frosty today. I say: leave it out Grace.

At lunch I sit again with Eber Petrelli and we dig into chickpea burgers in yellow tubs. He has a towel over his shoulders and shirt half unbuttoned. I ask him about his morning. He says: overall another resounding success but one technical problem just now with the lighting, didn't quite give us enough time to get through the final Exit Door concealed. Elena was mad, mad I tell ya. She almost bit that techie's head off. Sammy? I say. That's it, he says, I've never seen anything like it and remember I worked with Jean O'Connor during her crack days.

I spend the rest of lunch searching for Elena. I find her in History of Terror Part Two, which is all about the life and death of Amita Choudrey, The Red Widow. Elena is at the back of the cinema with a bag of Pick & Mix from The Kiosk. The projector splices CCTV footage of actual Amita entering Holden Tower after getting off the tube at Baker Street with grainy handheld film of young Ami in the paddling pool with her older brother and her budgie-smuggler father. Grew up in Berkshire. Pet rabbit called Jonesy. Broke arm at Butlins. Appendix out at eleven. University in Bristol, embarrassed in a mortar board. Met Adam Morey, a converted muslim. Went travelling. Rwanda, Uganda, Somalia. They marry, aged twenty-three. Morey dies. And then: before anybody knows it she's commanding an all-female mujahid terror squad in Somalia. Returns to the UK. Holden Tower falls at an angle, compressing into the ground. Elena eats her Pick & Mix like a child at the actual cinema. She sits there drinking it all in, again and again. She looks so fragile all of a sudden. How old is she? Jesus we didn't even use-.

I feel sick.

I run to the public loos.

I am sick in the public loos.

I have to walk through the Gift Shop to get back to the Staff Area. There are kids browsing the Holden Tower Dress-Up Collection. They can choose from Mini Amita, Mini Raymond, Mini Hostage, Mini Firefighter, and so on.

I am sick in the public loos again.

Must have been that chickpea burger.

Note: complain to Catering today.

She shoots me in the stomach ten more times that afternoon all quick and dirty and with each death I become less responsive, on my knees before long staring at her with sullen eyes and wishing, just wishing, that the bullet was real and the blood wasn't from a Blood Pack and that death was once again actual death, namely: final, crushing, irrevocable.

And then I get home and there's noone there.

Just a pink post-it which reads: Sammy told me.

I get in the empty bath and I cry until there are enough tears to drown in. I call but there is no answer. I keep calling to no avail. I think: well at least I'll get to watch some more episodes of Geia Mysteries on Demand. And then I hate myself for thinking that. I really do. I say out loud: you are truly a horrible human being. On the 89th time of trying I finally get through to her sister, Carrie, who informs me that they're all congregated at their mums bungalow in Watford. Carrie has driven down from Manchester especially for this family drama. They're having pizza and then watching that new Hank Lepsum film which she knows I hate. Sister-in-law begins to lay into to me but soon enough Sally-Ann grabs the phone. Angry But Somewhat Composed Wife: we're going to work this out and I'm going to try and understand what you've done and try to find it in my heart to love and trust you again, and I'm only going to do this for Mavis because she needs a father even if he is a good for nothing slab of horse shit. I'm sorry, I say, I wasn't myself I'm so sorry. Under one condition, she says: Daniel, you're to get a proper job.

Richard Fifield

Richard Fifield is a novelist and teacher, who lives in Missoula, Montana, USA. He spends his days gardening, cleaning, and decorating; he is his own trophy wife. Richard is devoted to his beloved dogs, Blanche, Oscar, and Frank. *You Can't Always Get What You Want* is inspired by his twenty years working as a case manager for developmentally disabled adults. The story was written in a doctor's office, while he waited for a friend. Richard is represented by Jenny Bent of The Bent Agency, and his debut novel, *The Flood Girls*, will be published by Gallery Books in 2015.

You Can't Always Get What You Want

The graveyard Staff sleeps on the couch, even though he isn't supposed to. The Nurse sleeps at her desk at her station. Dot likes telling on people, but won't ever rat them out. The group home is still from 2AM until 6AM. Just Dot and respirators, sleep apnea machines, humidifiers and snoring.

Dot watches Stuart sleep. Nurses put him to bed on his side, rotate him different nights, preventing bed sores. He has cerebral palsy and doesn't talk. She touches his penis through the bed sheet until it is hard. Dot feels better. Stuart has a colostomy bag, a wheelchair. Dot is fixated on his accessories, like a Barbie. She used to push his wheelchair, until staff had put a stop to it. Staff sang You Can't Always Get What You Want and took away her jigsaw puzzle. Dot had thrown a card table at the group home manager. Felt better.

Dot is always hungry. Staff lock all of the food in the outside pantry, because of Dot and MaryAnn. They both have Prader-Willi Syndrome, twins, squished heads, narrowed temples, elongated faces, noses too large, no lips to speak of. Tiny heads on giant bodies, shaped like Christmas trees. They are brittle diabetics, morbidly obese, and so they live in a medical group home because of this wrenching, painful hunger. Being bad makes Dot feel better. Not MaryAnn. Staff are nice to MaryAnn because she can't speak, and does not destroy things.

Last year, Staff had decided that MaryAnn would be Stuart's girlfriend, and Dot hates this. Staff had decided Stuart and MaryAnn were meant to be together, because they were both in wheelchairs, both incapable of speech. Staff coo when they are pushed next to each other, wheels locked. Matchmaking keeps Staff from boredom. MaryAnn sometimes puts her hand on Stuart's knee at day services, where they are supposed to put insulated socket sealers in cellophane bags. Staff take Stuart and MaryAnn out for movie dates, make them Valentines and Christmas Cards, purchase matching sweaters. Dot thinks this is unfair. MaryAnn is just as hungry, but is quiet about it. Dot is balding, knows she is not pretty. MaryAnn has all of her hair and perfect teeth. MaryAnn is an angel. Nurses aren't afraid of her. Dot and MaryAnn sit at the dining room table every night and do jigsaw puzzles and make necklaces. Staff only wear the ones that MaryAnn makes.

Staff hate Dot, because she is the only client that can talk, and tells on them for smoking weed in the bathrooms, for not wearing their seatbelts in the van, for calling John the Triple Winner, because he is deaf, blind and retarded. Including John, there are seven clients. Slattery lives in a jungle room, steamy with his humidifier, respirator and giant potted plants. Duane and Jacob both wear helmets for drop seizures. Dot enjoys their hallucinations.

Staff count out carbohydrates, fill measuring cups for Dot and MaryAnn, track the data on a clipboard for the Nurse. Every meal, Dot screams that they are being cheated, that the measuring cup is not full to the brim. Always, Staff sing You Can't Always Get What You Want, and Dot tries to scratch them, but Staff are fast at meal time.

Last week, Dot scooped the goldfish from the tank while the graveyard staff slept. Put them in the microwave, brought the dried out bodies to MaryAnn's bedroom for a midnight snack. Dot never shares, but MaryAnn is her only friend. The next morning, Staff sang You Can't Always Get What You Want, and Dot ripped the aquarium out of the wall, pulled a chunk of hair from the new Staff. Felt better.

For the next three days, Dot had refused her range of motion programs, refused her meds from the Nurse, tore all of the posters from her walls, and punched a hole in the sheetrock. Felt better. Staff sang You Can't Always Get What You Want and punished Dot by removing everything in her room but the bed and dresser of clothes. Dot piled all of her clothes in the center of the room and urinated on them. Felt better. Staff locked up her clothes outside, just like the food.

Today is Stuart's birthday, and Dot is caught stealing food from Duane's plate. Staff make her eat in the kitchen, sing You Can't Always Get What You Want. Staff light candles and pop balloons to startle Duane and Jacob, and Dot takes advantage of the distraction and eats from the garbage can. Feels better.

Time for cake. Staff are hyper-vigilant as they pass out the paper plates, watch Dot like a dangerous zoo animal. After cake, Dot decides to kiss Stuart on the lips. Staff yell at her. He is not your boyfriend. He is not your boyfriend. You Can't Always Get What You Want. Dot calls Stuart a fucking retard, and is sent her to her room.

Staff sit in a chair and keep watch outside her bedroom, and sing that song as Dot demolishes her empty dresser, as particle board splinters and flies when she throws the drawers against the unbreakable window. Feels better. The walls in her bedroom have already been cratered.

That night, Dot waits until the graveyard Staff and Nurse are asleep. She creeps to the bulletin board, removes two handfuls of thumbtacks. In Stuart's room, he is so handsome in the moonlight. As usual, he is on his side, face toward the wall.

She dumps the thumbtacks on the bed, and pulls him flat on his back. His eyes spring open, widen with pain. Silent tears as he shakes, but he cannot make a sound. Dot has saved one thumbtack, pokes a hole in his colostomy bag. After she closes his door, she feels better.

Sometimes, she finds she gets what she needs.

Amaryllis Gacioppo

Amaryllis Gacioppo is a writer from the Northern Rivers region
of NSW, Australia. In 2012 she received a BA with Honours
from the University of Technology, Sydney. Since graduating
she has spent her time travelling and slowly accumulating a
mass of words she likes to refer to as a novel. Her stories have
found homes in numerous journals and anthologies, including
Going Down Swinging, Two Serious Ladies, Grey Sparrow and
the *UTS Writers' Anthology*. Currently she is pursuing a PhD
in Creative Writing at Monash University in Melbourne.

Days

She'd said something to me the day before she did it. She called from a hotel in Nob Hill. She said: I think I might be better.

You never think you will be, and then one day you are.

I make my way out of the hostel, turning deaf against the usual hobo harangue, up Larkin Street to the cable car. How quickly the shock of the Tenderloin's teeming homeless population has worn off. A person suddenly is not a person – they're just somewhere below termites but above rain. She probably never came to this part of town. When she was here she lived in the Marina, where family money found friends.

I remember the photo of the house in one letter she sent, beach holiday blue-and-white with big bay windows, a piece of paper taped over the street number to ward off any questions or surprises. The years succeeding her departure were peppered with letters. She wrote that you could see the Golden Gate Bridge from the house, and to just try and show her a better orange than a California orange. With the chance I would have seen her California orange and raised her a Sicilian, but the absence of a return address was enough to call her bluff. When Dad told me what had happened, I thought: there it is. The final jilt of Mother Damned-est. A few weeks later the postman heralded the arrival of a battered Nespresso machine box with Dad's name scrawled on the side in permanent marker.

Nestled inside was a scrap of paper – an inventory for our consolation prize. Each item had been ticked off by her marauder, a gesture akin to counting out the notes to assure a debtor that the money's all there. Like this made us square. Here was her silk nightgown, her blue dress, a photo of the three of us in a silver frame, her wedding ring and some perfume that was different to the perfume she'd always worn when we knew her. Here was her gold-plated compact. Two wax California-orange-shaped candles. I made a habit of wearing the perfume. It was like making the acquaintance of someone I'd never known.

At the cable car stop, a man wearing a large khaki coat with the elbows duct-taped comes over. Hey baby, what are you doing tonight?

He says; Hey, I was talking to you. Hey! You don't have to be rude. Fuck you. I'm not some bum. I got a house, I got a job. I asked you a question.

A cable car churns to a halt at the stop and I get on. The duct-taped man gets smaller as the car pulls away; his tiny arms waving furiously like one of those angry characters in comic strips. The cable car passes by painted ladies and grocers. I don't know what I expected. But it sure looks different to the Saharan suburbia of the America in my childhood. I think: if this is the tornado in Texas, then the butterfly flapped its wings in Phoenix.

The reason I'm in San Francisco is because of Big Surf. This water park in Phoenix, Arizona where the American branch of our family reside. I was eleven. You clung onto inflatable donuts while artificial waves crashed over you and imported white sand strung itself along the lining of your swimmers, just like at a real beach except with no fish and way more pee. I'd gotten lost and he'd offered to lift me up onto his shoulders so I could spot them in the crowd. She saw me first: my head a bobbing beacon over the mechanical waves. She'd swum over, angry brushstrokes, the primal maternal instincts in her making a rare appearance, jabbing him with a finger and baring her teeth: What do you think you're doing with *my* kid buddy?

This was my mother. What a poker aficionado would call a maniac. Always raising the stakes, no matter how weak her hand. I guess she told herself she wanted to win, but really what she was after, when she launched herself headfirst into whatever came before her, was to kick up the dust, to thrill and be thrilled, to feel the blood rush hot in her veins.

It was one of those scenes in a movie, where there's a misunderstanding and then he blushes and stutters and clarifies, and then the sassy single mother laughs and then he laughs and the laughter is the sound of barriers shedding, barriers which the mother's had to build up around her because life is unkind, and also they're each realising how attractive the other one is. Except she wasn't single and when she brought him back over to where Dad and our family were, I felt my stomach drop because I knew that we were in for it again. *Look at the new friend I made!* And when they dizzily recounted, taking turns at starting and finishing sentences, I saw the way Dad looked at me, kind of like he was about to cry, kind of like he was about to rip his hair out by the roots, or mine, or both. And what I'm trying to say here is that you don't have to tell me something I already know. I could see the blood on my hands.

The cable car pulls up right near the mouth of the bridge. I step off into fog so thick that it's like wading through a cloud. Maybe she thought she was so close to heaven at the time that taking a single step would have brought her straight there; maybe she thought that resurrection would see her floating up amidst the fog, her soul doing breaststroke through the vapour.

She'd sent me a book after she left, a tacky souvenir one meant for kids, with gaudy drawings of the bridge being built and then the bridge through the decades since its erection. It was filled with fun facts and quizzes and I liked flipping through the pages and seeing the cars change models and the people change outfits. Facts like: *To hold its colour the Golden Gate Bridge is constantly re-painted, and when the bridge-painters get to one side they begin again from the other.* Another went something like: *In the twenties the only way across the bay from Sausalito to San Francisco was by ferry.* Seeing it in the flesh, the beams and cables are like the strung arteries of some poor colossus.

If I could print a new edition of that book I would make a few inclusions. Facts like: *There are more suicides on the Golden Gate than there are in any other place in the world.* Or if you want to get pretty about it: *People from all corners of the country specifically come to this place to end their lives, submerged in the glorious San Francisco Bay.* There's a thing called an Instinctive Drowning Response that is supposed to happen to a person whether they intend to drown or not. The prolonged restriction of air to the lung cavities will induce an autonomic reaction of panic in a drowning person, as the body's fight for breath overrides mental will. It's only a few minutes in, when the body's accepted that there's no chance for another breath, that the panic stops and the real drowning starts.

She'd spent her life treading water. Her state medals were strung along the walls in our hallway, her trophies glinting soldiers in phalanx form on the mantelpiece. She liked to swim in the lake near our house, her seaweed hair tucked up into a pink rubber cap. She said it was the only thing that kept her sane when she was pregnant with me and she didn't listen to the doctor when he told her to stop in the last few weeks. I was born in water, but I never took to it like she did. My earliest memories are in that lake, her smile wavering through the ripples as I splashed and bobbed, graceless, her voice tying up into a knot.

When it came to her final swim she'd thought ahead: stones in pockets, weights in shoes. I wonder where exactly on the bridge she did it. Whether she still wore the lipstick that made her look like she'd been sucking on a cherry lollypop. Her brandy cream skin. Her waterlogged body somewhere beneath me, like some miniature wrecked ship in a fish tank.

Time made evident her preferences. She liked them a certain age, for one thing. And while she might argue their differences, it was their supposed distinctions that betrayed them as carbon copies of one another. When I was two she ran off for a year to Europe with a professional swimmer, apparently in order to help him train for the Olympics. When I was seven it was a Peruvian Flamenco dancer for four months. Those were the longest stints. My childhood was peppered with discarded men or men who discarded her, the carpenter who reminded her of Jesus, the exhausting actor who'd butter me up with card tricks, the pathetic musician who wailed on his guitar out the front of our house after she'd left him. It all got to be quite interchangeable, right down to the precursor of the telltale signs: hushed phone conversations, alien cars parked in the driveway. Mum suddenly feeling wonderful and buying expensive outfits or discovering innate talents for cooking and guitar. Coming home to the house filled with 300 pink tulips one day and the next to Dad informing me Mum had fled the coop. And then an unforeseeable number of afternoons later, Mum's suitcase would be flung by the door, and she'd be upstairs in bed, crying into Dad's chest, clutching fistfuls of his shirt. Once we had to go pick her up from a suitor's love nest: a mangy little cottage on acreage at the edge of town. The first thing I remember seeing as we drove towards her was the hem of her dusty pink skirt performing acrobatics in the breeze. Mum waiting by the side of the road with giant sunglasses on, her hair flipping across her face and sticking to her lipstick. Her suitcases walled up around her, face obstinate but always glamorous. Dad muttering: Buck up, kiddo.

I walk the length of the bridge and keep going along the trail, collecting flowers along the way. At Vista Point I uncurl my hand and let the papery clusters of the pink sea thrifts, the bulbous heads of the leopard lilies, dip and dive into the sea. The tide ripples and laps at the base of the bluff. I watch out for plunging bodies, for a whirlwind of long hair and a discreet disturbance of water. I imagine her face emerging, ice-blue and glistening. A mess of wet hair. She never went in the water without her cap.

Always swimming or drowning. Drowning came after, when she came back to us and spent weeks in bed with the big gilt mirror propped up on her thighs, plucking hairs out of the crown of her head. Dad would play 'Guilty' by Russ Columbo and I'd peek through the crack in the door and he'd be leading her in a waltz around the bedroom. I knew he'd gotten her right again, breathed life back into her, when she picked up her feet instead of dragging them. I start on my way back to the other side of the bridge. I can smell the moss and the damp.

You can't tame a wild animal. That's the way Dad put it. By the time he found her, her Olympian dreams crushed – not for any kind of injury or melodrama, just because she was good but others were better – she was ready to be swept up. She was struggling to stay afloat and the arm he extended was a life raft. And I guess he liked that, being the rescuer. Every time she got towed under over the years, he was there to guide her back to shore.

I follow the Bay Trail, along the headlands and down to the beach in Marina, the red looming towers of the Golden Gate gradually fading in the distance. Restored row-houses painted in bright blues, whites and yellows with shiny SUVs in the driveways keep watch over the bay with their glassy windowed eyes. I watch out for their house and wonder if he still lives here. Whether he got a replacement, wedged himself into a new family. I'd like to find his door and give him a piece of my mind. Say: We are accomplices in this, you and I. I let her fall into the tide, but you were the rip after the swell. Tell him: You dragged her too far out. Too far out to where she couldn't reach us. I'd like to call his house and hang up, for weeks and months, let *him* hang on the dial tone.

White egrets call and soar overhead. I look back over my shoulder at the bridge. The mist is so thick that the steel girders of the bridge become fine red threads. Gusts of wind rush in from the Pacific, and it makes my skin sticky with salt. Young dog-walkers clutch thick scarves to their necks and wear woollen jumpers and chase after unleashed clusters of puppies, frustrated, calling to Misty or Susie or Bella as the dogs tear through the dark, damp sand. One of them races over and I reach down to pat its head. The dog burrows its snout into the sand. It scratches at the water, the soft waves. To the end of our days, we would love her, loyal as a pair of dogs.

The last time I knew. He called himself an artist but 'usurper' would be more apt. He engulfed her and swept her away. When we got back to Australia we thought we were safe, the Pacific Ocean a seemingly staunch fortress. But he called and he called and Mum was floating and when he finally arrived it felt like a slow-moving tidal wave had finally come down upon us.

I lie back on my elbows and rake my fingers across the sand. The pink and purple fuchsias that sprout from the bushes hang over the dunes like exotic lampshades. My mind occasionally returns to the last time I saw her. She'd knelt down to me, scanned my face, her eyes never really looking, never really fixing themselves on the one spot. Over her shoulder, his silhouette by the door. What a joke. Even if he was there by his own admission, to 'make sure things didn't get out of hand', he'd have trouble breaking up a scuffle between two mice. He was there to hurt us more, to make sure we wouldn't change her mind. With her gaze fixed on Dad's feet, planted so firmly on the ground, his head in his hands, she grabbed my cheeks in one hand and said: You'll see when you're older.

There are some things you hope you'll never see or understand. But you can't control what you inherit. If you could pick, what would you choose

– a life of leaving or being left? The water is a dark grey now, almost black, and a sea hawk hovers above it before plunging into the water feet first, emerging with fins and tails flapping in its claws. The pink clouds glow and pulsate as the sun goes down. Men and women in suits on their way home from work stroll along the sand with their office shoes in their hands. The lights dotting the bridge smoulder in the dense mist that surrounds them. The air smells salty and full with the sea.

I retrace my steps through the streets of the Tenderloin, back through all the streets I walked this morning. Past a fenced-in park as the wind pastes discarded hamburger wrappers onto the bars of the iron gates. It's the kind of park where the chains on the swings are so rusted with age that the metal looks as if it will disintegrate into shrapnel at any moment and any number of insidious objects could be cradled in the overgrown grass: errant syringes, bent forks, broken light bulbs, a knife. Past a Vietnamese restaurant with one of those gaudy water features inside that have those massive goldfish swimming around in them and those purifiers that hum so loudly they seem to envelop all sound. Convenience stores with trays of bruised fruit out the front that has probably been rotting in those trays for god knows how long, fruit so ridden with secret mould that it would probably break apart in your hand the second your teeth hit the flesh. I grab pizza from a grubby hole-in-the-wall, the walls white and the floor white and the parmesan on the pizza white, the slices as greasy as the man behind the counter's hair and congealing in humming bain-maries.

In Arizona the kids would play in the pool out back, taking turns jumping off the diving board and crashing into the water's surface. My cousin would play a game where he would grip my shoulders and head from behind and push me down below the water, seeing for how long he could stand on my back, while I struggled to throw him off, my face jammed against the fibreglass floor of the pool. There was the last time, the time when he pushed down too long. My head and chest felt as if they would burst with blood and cold. The water was heavy and thick. When a person is having an Instinctive Drowning Response, there is a kind of trigger that stops it. While submerged, a person will hold their breath for as long as possible before surrendering to the breathing reflex. Eventually the reflex takes over and water will gush into the airways instead of breath. Water doesn't fill up in the lungs as you might think though. The body is smart. Laryngospasm is what happens when a person's body detects fluid in the lung cavities and the air tubes seal up. It's your stomach that fills up with water instead. This is when the panic falls away and the good stuff sets in. This is the thing that no one expects – that succumbing is bliss. You're freed of pain and it's as if you are floating. You shed the need to breathe, and before you lose consciousness, it is like you are cocooned inside a cloud. The next thing I remember is the hot concrete on my back, black and white dots speckling the clear sky, both my mother's and cousin's tear-streaked faces, the convulsing of my chest as I heaved chlorinated water onto the concrete. The blood-flow rushing back up to my skin, bursting capillaries like tiny ants rummaging through my arteries: big, big breaths.

The street lamps are muddy crystal balls. I can smell jasmine and the mint from the Vietnamese around the corner. The city lights are like embers, the sky aflame with a violet haze, and I wonder where all the days go, all the days of my youth that already seem so far away, all the days behind me. There is the taste of blood in my cheeks. Letting go is the hardest part, but once you do, the drowning is easy.

Sophie Hampton

Sophie Hampton has had work broadcast on BBC Radio 4 and published in *Southword*, *The London Magazine*, *The View From Here*, *The Yellow Room*, the *Eastern Daily Press* and *Scribble* magazine.

Competition success includes winning the Sean O'Faolain International Short Story Prize, *The London Magazine* Short Story Competition and the *Eastern Daily Press* Short Story Competition, 2nd Prize at the Wells Festival of Literature and shortlistings for various prizes including the Bridport Prize and the Fish Short Story Prize. Sophie has an MA (Distinction) in Creative Writing from Sheffield Hallam University for which she received the AM Heath Prize. She is currently editing her debut collection of short stories.

The Tower

Hippo *Birdie Two Ewe!* Inside my only card Nan has written *Guess what we're doing today? I'll meet you in the car park at 12.* I study the picture on the front: a hippopotamus, a budgie and two sheep.

Mum shuffles into the kitchen. The stains on her nightie match the stains on the table cloth: egg yolk, ketchup, oil. She lights a cigarette and scrunches up the box, aims for the bin. Spaz shot. I finish my cocoa puffs and slurp the chocolatey milk from my bowl. I like chocolate milk but the milk we drink at school makes me gag in summer when it's warm.

'I could do with a cup of tea,' says Mum.

I strike a match and switch on the gas. Mum won't light the stove. She's scared of an explosion, like the one at Ronan Point. She hates living in the sky. 'I'm not a bloody bird,' she says, but she looks like one with her skinny legs and sparrow-brown hair and dark eyes.

As I wait for the kettle to boil I clear a space on the windowsill for my card.

'Are you really eleven?' Mum says. 'You make me feel old. Is that from Nan?'

I nod.

'I tried to get you one yesterday. Lazy bastard shut the shop early.'

The sky is grey as wet pavements, the same colour as the tower block opposite. A red shirt drifts past our window, arms flapping, followed by the whoosh and blur of a rubbish sack. The chute's full - the dustmen are on strike - and it's dangerous to stick your head outside. Mark Taylor got hit by a beer can.

'Scum,' says Mum.

The kettle whistles and I take it off the stove. 'Nan's taking me out today. Got any money?'

'Not till Monday. I'll borrow some though, get something nice for tea.'

'Surprise!'

Mum and I jump.

Nan has let herself in. She never comes up to our flat, says it's too depressing. She's wearing the brown dress with pink flowers that she bought on the market and her special-occasion turquoise eye shadow.

'Happy birthday, sweetheart.' She pants hot minty breath on my cheek as she kisses me. 'Thought I'd never make it. The lift packed up on the tenth floor.'

'Where are you taking her?' says Mum.

'Did you guess?' says Nan. 'From my card?'

'No,' I say.

'The zoo! We're going to the chimps' tea party!'

'Wow!'

'Waste of money,' says Mum, as she taps ash into my cereal bowl. 'I wouldn't pay to see some bloody monkeys.'

'You've got no money left after your fags and liquorice torpedoes,' says Nan. 'No wonder your teeth are rotten.'

'Least I've still got my own,' says Mum. Her cigarette sizzles when she stubs it out. 'I'm going back to bed.'

Nan and I walk along the landing where Mr Gazillion, our neighbour, is at his front door.

'Morning,' says Nan but Mr G turns his back on us. His shoulder blades stick out from his white shirt like the peaks on a circus tent.

Mr G's got elephant ears and lips that have folded in on themselves and sucked-in cheeks where wrinkles run as deep as rivers. He must be older than a hundred. Mark said that gazillion is the biggest number in the universe so that's why I call Mr G what I do.

Mr G spies on me. He knows what time I leave for school – he comes to his door just as I walk past – even if I'm late. *Morning* I say and he grips the bars over his door and stares like an animal or puts his hands on the sides of his head and peeps through his fingers. He must press his ears against the walls to find out when I'm leaving. I bet he can hear everything: his earholes are big and dark as caves and the walls are thin, so thin that I can hear him peeing from my bedroom. He pees a lot. Mark says that when you're old you piss yourself and shit yourself and dribble like a baby.

The door shuts and he's gone.

'Charming,' says Nan.

'Mr Gazillion can't talk. He's lost his teeth.'

'You don't need teeth to talk. What's his real name?'

'He hasn't got one. Doesn't need it. He doesn't know anybody apart from me and Meals on Wheels.'

'Your mum had the baby blues so bad that you didn't have a name for 42 days. If I hadn't marched her to the registry office you wouldn't have one now.'

'Oh,' I say and frown. I wish Nan hadn't told me that. Especially on my birthday.

If I have a daughter I'm going to spoil her with names: Susan Leslie Ursula - unless I marry Mark Taylor. Imagine the graffiti. Mark's in the second year at the comprehensive and he looks smart in his navy trousers and his shirt and tie. My cheeks go hot when I think about him. It would be good to have a husband seeing as neither Mum nor Nan has. He could do some DIY.

The sun's out when we get off the bus so I tie my cardigan around my waist. Nan finds a lump of bubble gum stuck to her dress and goes in a bad mood. I expect the gum got there when she was in the lift because she leant against the wall; you should never lean against the walls: sometimes the pee is still wet.

'How disgusting,' she says. She tries to pull the gum off with a piece of toilet roll but it gets tufts stuck in it.

'Nobody will notice,' I say. 'It's the same colour as the flowers.'

She tuts and walks faster. Her backside wobbles because her heels are too high.

Regent's Park is posh; there are no travellers' camps or prowling dogs like in London Fields. Nan buys two tickets for the tea party. I try to forget the cost in case Mum asks and gets cross. Nan and I have Mr Whippy's; by the time I have eaten the flake the ice cream is already melting.

We squeeze onto the end of a bench near the front of the audience. When I sit down my dress pulls up over my knees; the label says age 9 but it's the only dress I had which was clean. The girl next to me, all tanned and blonde with ribbons in her hair, narrows her blue eyes. Glistening in the sun, the gum on Nan's dress looks as though it is still covered in spit.

The zookeeper, who is wearing a black suit and has sweat dripping from under his cap, brings out four chimpanzees and leads them to a platform where a table has been set. The animals climb onto their chairs and pick up cutlery except the smallest chimp who refuses to face the table and rocks backwards and forwards. He puts his hands on his head and, like

Mr Gazillion, peers through his fingers. The chimps drink cups of tea and munch on fruit except the smallest who doesn't eat anything. When the zookeeper pours tea over the smallest chimp's head everyone laughs except me. People stop laughing when a chimp jumps off his chair and throws a lump of poo into the crowd.

I don't like the tea party but I don't tell Nan because it's kind of her to bring me. The chimps remind me of Mr G - his dull eyes and flat nose and turned-in lips and wrinkles - even though the chimps are young and Mr G is ancient. When a chimp flings his iced bun on the ground I think it's wrong for the animals to have a party when poor Mr G has to eat Meals on Wheels on his own and I won't even have a birthday cake.

I'm pleased when it's over. Nan waits with me in the queue for the bus. 'Sit upstairs at the front,' she says, as she hands me my fare. 'You might get away without paying.'

Mark and two other boys are kicking a ball against the NO BALL GAMES sign.

'Happy birthday!' Mark yells.

John and Patrick make kissy noises and my cheeks burn.

'Where've you been?' says Mark. 'I knocked for you.'

'Nan took me to the zoo. To the chimpanzee's tea party.'

'OOH OOH OOH AH AH AH!' he screeches.

Patrick pretends to pick fleas from John's hair.

'You know John's got nits?' says Mark.

'Ugh!' says Patrick and whacks John over the head. John rolls across the ground, leaps up and chases Patrick through the car park.

'Did you get money for your birthday?' asks Mark.

'No.'

'Any presents?'

'The zoo was my present from Nan and Mum.'

'I wanted to get you something. I tried to nick some sweets but Parker nabbed me. You should try. Girls can get away with anything. Short dress like that. Everyone knows Parker's a fuckin' perv. He keeps a porno mag under the till. I saw a tit poking out once.'

My cheeks burn hotter. 'Stealing's wrong,' I say.

'No, it ain't. We ain't got nothing. Our mums ain't got nothing.'

My heart beats fast. Mark puts his hands on my shoulders. 'You're roasting,' he says. 'Hot for me, are you?'

'I got sunburnt at the zoo.'

'I dare you to nick some sweets,' says Mark. 'Everyone does it. Buy some chews and nick some chocolate.' He takes two shiny new half pennies from his trousers.

The coins glint in the sun. I can taste the stench of used nappies coming from the mountain of rubbish. The tinkle of an ice cream van grows louder until the chimes ring inside my head. A group of girls chant in the playground ... *to fetch a pail of water. Poor old Jill forgot her pill and came down with a daughter.*

'Or are you chicken?' says Mark.

My name is Elvis Presley, girls are sexy, sitting on a balcony ...

'Look at me,' Mark says.

'I'm not chicken.'

He gives me the coins. His hand is sweaty. I tug down my dress as I walk across the estate.

I say hello to Mr Parker who nods and returns to his football pools. As I wander along the aisle I slip two bars of chocolate into my pocket. At the counter I pick a couple of Black Jacks from the box. 'Just these please, Mr Parker.'

He wipes his hands on his grubby white coat, takes the money and puts it in the till. 'How's your mum? I haven't seen her for a while.'

'Says she's feeling old. It's my birthday.'

'Happy birthday! Here ... ' He rummages in the Fruit Salad box and tips a handful into my palm.

'Thank you.' I glance under the till. No sign of tits.

'Easy!' I say. I give Mark a bar of chocolate.

'Wow! Flash your knickers, did you?'

'I just took it off the shelf. Mr Parker gave me some chews as well.'

Mark looks so impressed. He rips the wrapper off. 'Race you!'

The chocolate is already soft. We gobble down a bar each, biting off square after square without stopping. My throat feels gloopy and it's hard to swallow.

Mark! Mark! Mark! A sound like a bird cheeping. We strain our necks upwards. Mark's mum is leaning out of their kitchen window on the sixteenth floor, small as a doll, hair yellow as custard. 'Tea's ready!'

When the lift stops for me to get out, the doors open but Mark presses the button and closes them again. He pins me against the wall. I think of the pee stains and the gum on Nan's dress. He kisses me and I don't stop him. It's quick and dry and hard and smells of sunshine and chocolate.

I stumble along the landing, heart thumping. Mr Gazillion is waiting at his door. He sticks his hand through the bars and holds out an envelope.

'For me?' I say. 'Thank you. How did you know it was my birthday?'

He smiles his lipless smile and stares, the whites of his eyes so dull and bloodshot that they are hardly white at all.

I unlock the door and kid myself that Mum's gone to buy food for tea. I open Mr G's card. It says *Happy Birthday to Someone Special* above a picture of a girl with dark hair twirling a hula hoop. He hasn't written anything inside. The card makes me sad because if Mr G knew what I had just done in the shop and in the lift he wouldn't think that I was special. But I put it on the windowsill next to Nan's because on its own her card looks lonely.

I steal every time Mum sends me to buy something from the shop now. I feel bad but it serves Mr Parker right because he charges rip-off prices and Mark's so nice to me when I show him what I've stolen. I nick chocolate and sweets or, if I've got my school bag, crisps and biscuits and cans of pop.

'You're a natural,' says Mark. 'You should have a go in Woolies.'

'Wouldn't dare. I only get away with it because Mr Parker knows me.'

Mark makes out with me whenever we're in the lift. I don't like it as much as on my birthday because he pushes his tongue inside my mouth and his kisses are wet and squelchy. Once he put his hand up the front of my tee shirt, like he'd find anything there, and I was so relieved when Mrs Aldridge from our landing got in. I'm too scared to stop Mark doing stuff because Debra Hardy fancies him and even though she's only twelve, Patrick told me that she's gone all the way.

'You know that Debra nicks from Woolies,' says Mark one evening. 'If you'd pinch stuff I'd sell it. We'd split the cash and buy anything we want. John's brother can get us fags. You'd be better off smoking. You're getting fat.'

'I'm not getting fat!' I say.

I examine myself in the mirror when I get home. I undo my trousers and there are marks where the waistband has been digging into my skin. My tummy sticks out a bit too. 'Fat thief,' I say to my reflection. Tears trickle down my cheeks which are chubbier than they used to be. 'Fat, slutty, thief.'

Debra's tits have grown even bigger and she wears low cut tops. When

Mark's around she pretends to drop things so that she has to bend down. Thinking about her keeps me awake at night. I hear Mr Gazillion get up and pee and the whoosh of the flush. I hear the cough that rattles his body and makes his bed springs creak. I don't want him to know that I'm a thief. I worry that his elephant ears can hear me and Mark when the hot wind swirls around the estate and carries our voices up the stairwells and through the corridors and along the landings before it blows them over the balconies and safely into the muffle of the clouds.

'Surprise!' I say on Saturday afternoon. I pull five number one singles from underneath my cardie, and a bag of pick 'n' mix from my pocket, and hand them to Mark.

'You are the best,' he says. And he kisses me on the lips and squeezes my bum. In the middle of the playground. In front of Patrick and John and Debra. The tower blocks march across the sky.

A man moves away from a window on the twelfth floor.

On Monday morning I try on three dresses before I find one that's not too short and tight. I put the kettle on for Mum's tea. I take the cereal box from the cupboard but all that's left are the dusty bits at the bottom so I have cream crackers with marge and jam.

'Your dress is too small,' Mum says when I take in her drink. She's sitting up in bed eating liquorice torpedoes, her tongue black as a slug.

'It's not my fault I'm growing! There's a jumble sale in the church on Saturday. If you give me a bit of child allowance I'll buy myself some clothes.'

'There's none left.'

'You only collected it the other day.'

'I owed money.'

'There's nothing to eat.'

'That's why you get free school dinners. Here, have one of these.' She offers me the bag of liquorice.

Halfway along the landing I stop and turn. Mr Gazillion isn't at his front door. Mr G has been at his door as I leave for school every day since we moved in two years ago. I wait for a few minutes, kicking at the mushrooms which grow in cracks in the concrete.

A gust of wind snatches petals from the geraniums in Mrs Aldridge's window box. *Please let Mr G come out before the petals land.* I lean over the balcony until the flowers, like red butterflies, flutter out of sight. Still no Mr G.

A wrecking ball, which in the distance looks no bigger than a gobstopper, swings from a crane. The ball crashes into the side of a factory but all I can hear is the thud of my heart. A white dust cloud rises from the ground and I watch it until it disappears. I glance at Mr G's door and window and check the time: five to nine. I hurry along the landing.

I run home after school, as fast as I can while avoiding the pavement cracks. *If I don't tread on the cracks he'll be there.* Mr G's door is shut. I press my face against the bars but I can't see through the net curtain at the window.

'You just ran straight past me!'

I jump. Mark scowls at me. He must have followed me up.

'Sorry,' I say. 'I'm worried about Mr G. He wasn't at his door this morning.'

'He's probably gone out for the day.'

'He doesn't go out. He gets Meals on Wheels.'

'Have you tried ringing his bell?'

'No.'

'Why not?'

'Because I'm scared he doesn't answer.'

Mark rolls his eyes. He presses the buzzer. Holds his finger down.

'He's not there,' I say.

Mark continues to ring the bell.

'Stop it!'

Mark shakes the metal gate. To my surprise it opens. He tries the handle of the door and that opens too.

I gasp.

'Coming?' he says.

'No! He might be dead.'

'Someone's got to find him.'

The flat smells of hospital and shepherd's pie. Mark switches on the light; it glows dull yellow through a dust-covered bulb. We creep along the hallway which has the same lino as ours.

The door to the lounge is open. Mr Gazillion is sitting on a green velour sofa, his back to us, his neck so scrawny that his spine runs up the middle like a broom handle wrapped in skin. He is staring at the photographs on the chimney breast. When a sheet of peeling wallpaper rustles in the draft from the front door I jump and knock against a vase on the bookcase. I try to grab the vase but it topples and smashes as it hits the ground. 'Oh!' I yelp. Mark sprints into the hallway.

Mr G doesn't flinch.

I've never seen a dead person in real life.

I didn't know that you could die sitting up.

Mr G lifts his hand to scratch one of his elephant ears and I scream.

Mark comes back in. 'What's going on? Shut the fuck up.'

'Don't swear in front of Mr G.'

'Fuck me!' says Mark, wide-eyed. 'He's deaf! He has no idea we're in here. Look ... ' He crouches behind the sofa. 'Hey, spastic!' he yells.

'Don't be so nasty. Let's go.'

'No way. We can nick anything. I'm going to check the bedroom.'

I follow him. 'Stop it.'

Mark lifts the mattress. 'Zilch,' he says. 'Except piss stains.' He turns to the chest of drawers, empties it of folded clothes.

'Leave his things alone.'

'Why? You never nicked anything?'

I pick Mr G's clothes off the floor. When I go back into the lounge, Mark is taking books, one by one, from the shelf. He fans through the pages and drops each book on the floor with a thud. When I grab his arm he shakes off my hand.

'Yeah!' he shouts. Dozens of banknotes flutter from a Bible: green, purple, brown. He gathers them up and stuffs them into his pockets. 'Thanks, mate,' he says to Mr G's back. 'Much appreciated.'

'You can't steal his money,' I say.

'Tell you what, I'll do a swap.' He unzips his flies.

I watch horrified as he pees into the soil of a spider plant. 'I'm going to find a policeman, tell him what you've done!'

'I'll pound you if you do,' Mark says, as he zips up his trousers. He gives me the finger and leaves, slamming the front door so hard that the walls shake. Flakes of plaster drift from the ceiling. Mr G turns and stares at me.

I try to say sorry but my voice doesn't work. The look in Mr G's eyes and the smell of pee make me retch. Mr G turns back to the photographs on the wall. He is no longer still. He rocks backwards and forwards like the chimpanzee.

When I smell burning that night I get out of bed and go to the balcony. Someone has set fire to the rubbish in the car park again. I listen to the crackle of the flames and watch the shadows of the rats as they flee the burning pile. I tiptoe to Mr G's door and try the gate but it's locked. I wait there until I hear a siren and the blue flashing lights close in.

I haven't seen Mr G since. I write him a letter each evening but I never put it through his door. Mark and Debra make out everywhere: in the stairwells, on the platform at the top of the slide, in the car park, watched by me and a down-and-out as she gulps from a bottle of meths.

One night I take a bucket of water and some rags into the lift to wash off the graffiti. Mark's spelling is rubbish: *fat and fridgid*. I wonder if anyone has dialled our telephone number to ask for *sluty sex with a slag*; the line was cut off ages ago, when Mum lost her job and stopped paying the bills. I rub the walls so hard that sweat trickles down my chest but the words don't even smudge.

We finish school at dinner time on the last day of term. On the way home I worry about being at the comp in September with Mark, Debra, Patrick and John. When I come out of the lift, Mum and Mrs Aldridge are chatting on the landing; Mum's knickers flap on the washing line above their heads.

Two men come out of Mr G's flat, the green velour sofa on their shoulders. I squeeze against the railings as they carry it past. The cushion on one side is sagging and worn.

'What's going on?' I ask Mum. 'Where's Mr G?'

'He's gone.' She takes a liquorice torpedo from the pocket of her nightie and pops it into her mouth.

James Hughes

James Hughes lives in Melbourne. His short stories have won a number of awards in Australia. In 2014 he was shortlisted for the Southword International Poetry Competition. He is also the winner of the 2013 John Shaw Neilson Poetry Prize. His articles sometimes appear in *The Melbourne Age, The Australian* and *The Big Issue*. He's written on hiking in South Korea, great book cover illustrations, Holocaust survivors living in Melbourne, the use of silence in films, the use of others' unwanted books, the forgotten genius of Joni Mitchell, the primitive cool of cricket legend Dennis Lillie and DH Lawrence's novel *Kangaroo*.

The Stone,
The Storm,
The End of Huckleberry Finn

Clearing my mother's shed recently I stumbled on a stray pack of Polaroids. I found my brother, sister and I in the bruise-blue ocean one Easter Sunday: Leo, slender as a fawn, bending to cup the froth; our younger sister, topless in board shorts, watching him, bemused; me charging an oncoming wave. The kind of unaffected photograph only a mother's lens could orchestrate. The kind of supposedly miscellaneous snap whose allure takes years to crystalize.

I nearly missed him, closer to camera on the wet sand.

Ears pegged back, front paw cocked, crooked tail afloat.

Our first dog was gaunt and tan with a sleepy pungent fart that made my sister cackle and my old man wince and frown over *The Herald*.

The days we were a family had him at their fragile axis.

When he leaned out of our sunburned station-wagon his liquorice pink and black lips flapped and his downy ears pinned back, exposing a maze of waxy grey bulbs and a tunnel that could only have led to his soul. I wanted to climb all the way through and become part of him.

My old man was short with a sturdy veneer and a gorgeous deep doomed laugh; a holder of the floor at barbecues and neighbourhood New Year's Eve parties; always making other men laugh, shaking a match in blue-grey fog.

At home he was always shaking his head, inventing reasons things couldn't be achieved.

Late the fourth night the dog was missing I stood behind the lounge room door and heard her accuse him of driving the dog away somewhere, of leaving him on the side of a road somewhere, to appease an old neighbour who was always complaining about his midnight moon songs.

"Never mind the happiness of your own children and family. So long as the neighbours aren't inconvenienced, I mean . . . God forbid." She sounded afraid of her words, afraid of their being true. "Isn't that what's happened?"

I pictured him staring out the blackened window.

She repeated the accusation.

He struck a match, tossed the box on the coffee table and said she was as mad as her sister had ever been.

Taut silence filled the room.

"Why won't you just admit what you've done?"

"Why won't you just leave me in peace?"

"You're planning to leave? Is that why you're doing this? This is your cruel and . . . cowardly way of preparing us?"

"*Eileen.*" He flipped ash into the heavy glass ashtray. "I did not *touch* that – dog."

"You haven't even the honesty. Why did you even have a family if you didn't want one?"

Seven days after the dog disappeared, my brother and sister and I burst open the car doors as our mother turned us into the driveway – the dog thrashed its tail spinning circles behind the gate! Dad was standing on the veranda, smoking, wearing his sunglasses. The dog was emaciated but he was alive and we were soaring at his side running to the park in the wind, singing his name for the neighbourhood.

We never found out where he'd been, or how he'd gotten home.

In a less chaotic world the animal's tribulations would have ended then and there.

A year later fortune dealt an even stranger, even more inscrutable hand.

My family has never talked about it.

She appeared one Sunday stuffing junk mail in letterboxes. (*I FOUND it at Fosseys!!!*) Her harried walk was out of step with the slanted, languid, lilting late afternoon light.

As she lifted the letterbox lid the dog nipped her hand.

My mother put down the hose, apologizing, asking her in.

"What and get savaged a second time?"

"Please . . . if you're hurt?"

"Some of us have to work." She traipsed to the next letterbox.

I'd seen her before: walking home from the bus stop, after school, sometimes I'd see her going up her concrete steps, lugging a green laundry basket stacked with grey school uniforms.

It was a drab house, I'd occasionally thought. A prison-grey front wall stood over a lifeless, clumpy front yard. Even the tough, patchy grass seemed begrudged by the dirt.

Close to the curb stood a stake. Nailed to the stake was the plastic lid of an ice cream container.

IRONING DONE
REASONABLE RATES

She decided to sue.

My brother and sister and I knew nothing of this.

Compensation litigation was the happening thing in Australia in 1985 but as a family, we were hardly fertile ground for its plough. My mother worked in a paint shop (*Bristol Colours Your World!*). My dad had started nightshift in a dairy with a neighbour, after losing his job as a salesman for a greeting card maker on the fringe of town. He'd told his father across the oceans he was doing a "night-time operational pasteurisation programme."

As a kid I had this habit: I'd stand in the hall, clandestine, listening to my parents slashing each other with words the way only the Irish can.

I knew it was wrong, but I was learning too much: I knew about his affair, about his never having wanted so many children, and other matters mainly to do with money – there was never enough and his interest in fixing this was null and void.

This time they weren't exactly arguing, but something was very wrong, and I couldn't tell what.

"She's going for our throats, Eileen." He inhaled Super Mild. "The bitch has us over a bloody barrel."

"I could ring Gran," she said, meaning her mother. "She'd lend us enough to get a solicitor."

He took a deeper, longer drag. "I've a feeling we've exhausted that option."

"Thanks to your – " She looked away.

"Thanks to my what?"

I felt him glare at her; felt him look away, at the darkened window.

I stood very still, staring at the slice of light between the base of the door and the carpet.

Our grandmother's clock went *tling*, ten times; the short-lived silences between each note encapsulating time's mystique.

He mumbled something grave. I leaned closer.

"I couldn't." Terrific sadness filled her voice. "I will not do that to these children."

"We might have to, Eileen." He stubbed his cigarette in the thick glass ashtray on the coffee table. "If that's the only way she'll stop craving her pound of flesh . . . we might have to."

"We can't just let a *stranger* do as she pleases with our lives – our children's lives."

"And would you prefer to be dragged through court and end up owing her money until the moon turns a nice shade of blue?"

In bed I lay awake. The dog slept at my feet, bamboozled by a dream.

At the end of the next school day I was surprised at the sight of dad waiting in the car at the school bus bays. (We caught the bus to and from school without fail.) As he saw me coming he touched the lenses of his Polaroids.

I went for the front seat and he told me to save it for my sister. When I asked what he was doing here he said he just felt like saving us the bus trip on a day this muggy.

Leo showed up looking dehydrated and drained after a hard day taunting teachers.

As our sister approached, hunched under her bag, dad turned the ignition. She took the front and he leaned to kiss her and the prickles of his beard touched her face.

As we spluttered out the gates she asked why the dog hadn't come for the ride. He stared at the road as if he hadn't heard.

She asked could we take him down the beach after tea, if it stayed hot.

He cocked his head away from her, to his open window, and shifting in his seat expelled smoke from his nostrils.

Warm air whipped around the backseat.

She leaned out her window and her hair fanned like a flame in a raging wildfire.

Stopped at the lights outside the Technical School, the ABC radio newsreader forecast a change with the chance of a storm. Silence filled the airwaves a long moment, as if he were giving everybody time to digest the information.

On the veranda we kicked off our shoes. Dad asked us to come into the lounge room, altogether.

"Why?" Leo peeled his sweaty socks. "Did we win Tatts?"

Dad closed the flywire; stood a few moments staring at a square of orange sun on the carpet, by the small square of stained glass beside the front door.

In the lounge we stood in front of the couch and he crouched.

His tone was subdued.

There was, he said, something he had to tell us.

He took a minute to explain.

The words were strangely benign.

My brother roared and left the room and kicked something off on the veranda. My sister couldn't make a sound. She just kept shaking her head ignoring his hands on her shoulders, ignoring whatever it was he was saying.

There was this ringing in my ears.

"Let me get this straight . . . because it sounds so piss-weak I can hardly believe it." Mick Reed stood with one sole on the curb and one on the baking bitumen. "She sent a letter saying she was getting up a court case –

now Huck's six-feet under." He scratched a nipple and looked at the fence.

"So your olds backed down to an ironing lady."

Leo, hunched beside me on the curb, flushing, stared at the bitumen in stony shame.

Reed shifted his weight and his soles traded places. "Somebody should pay her a little visit."

Neither Leo nor I answered him.

Reed bristled. "So dying in the arse is better is it?"

Leo stood up in sudden fury but only shot his friend a look.

The glowering sun pulsed.

"Good old Huck Finn." Reed shook his head. "What an absolutely piss-poor way to go out. If nobody pays her a little visit in the dark tonight, we'll have to wait until the dust clears, make a night of it."

Lying on the bottom-bunk in the broiling bedroom I disowned thoughts of the dog, drowned thoughts of the dog, dwelling at numbed length on the kind of immaterial minutiae we dwell on when our heart aches: a spindly wire in a light-globe, like a trapped stick-insect; an elongated scorch in the bunk's grain, like the head and beak of a bird; a patch of carpet turning orange in throbbing sun, turning tan again as the sun withdraws.

In my guts I felt the dog's name.

The dog's name came rising into my throat.

Barely audibly, I heard myself say it, and for an eerie moment, felt as if I might have only ever imagined him. Then the ringing again – annulling feeling.

I pictured going to the woman's house after dark, armed with a stone.

I pictured the window splintering. To shatter it with the requisite revenge, a stone would not be enough.

The stone became a brick.

A brick was too heavy to carry all that way. The brick became a stone again.

I hauled myself off the bed and left the bedroom.

From the fence inside the gate I took up the bike.

Outside her house I rolled circles on the road, listening to the spokes ticking.

On one side of her house, a neighbour's front garden bloomed and blossomed.

On the other side was a strangely blank quarter-acre block. No birds or even insects ever landed there. The only traces of life were grey-green thickets of thorns: one right in the middle and one in the back corner, nuzzling her grey, splintery fence.

In the corner of my eye I thought I saw the blinds budge in her front window.

I rolled away downhill and drifted left along unpaved Ruth Road feeling the tremors through the soles of my thongs.

I pulled up between two pines at the entrance to the old mini-bike track. On the other side a kid in an orange T-shirt lost ground in a tug-of-war with his dog.

In the harsh, thirsty grass by the bike's front wheel, a troupe of bull ants ferried a blazing green and orange Christmas beetle, upturned and still kicking. The ants stopped all at once as if unsure where exactly they were taking it. The beetle sensed the uncertainty, I was sure, but unless I helped it out, it was toast. As I glanced around me for a twig to set it free something spiky struck me hard about the ear – in one maladroit motion I ducked and lashed out with an arm. Flooding with adrenalin I kicked away from a fat magpie swinging around in a U taking affronted dutiful aim again.

Cutlery did the talking at the table.

The old man cleared his throat a few times, as if the sound explained things.

Our mother tried her best. Each of her words required strength and artifice. She'd made an awful compromise and knew it in her marrow.

Leo pushed his chair back without a sound and left. The wishbone lay pointlessly and stupidly on his plate.

The screen door closed limply behind him. I listened to his feet go down the veranda. The gate opened.

I listened to my dad chew.

I simmered. He chewed his chicken. I resented his eating: resented his being.

In his face I saw none of my own. In his cowardice I saw none of my own.

In twilight, in an empty garden, I resumed my never-ending private cricket tournament between imaginary countries: The Lower Regions of Eastern Nowhere: The Allied Tribes of New Caledonia Highlands. When I came around the back of the house looking for a wayward ricocheted ball, I came across the animal's big red water bowl. A baby mosquito floated face down. After gazing a curious stretch of time I picked up the half-empty bowl and carried it to the compost heap: watermelon rinds crawled with ants: the potato peelings had shrivelled since yesterday. The word felt strange, all at once . . . yesterday . . . yesterday.

I emptied his water with a sloppy splash and gnats rose startled from the stink.

The incinerator gave off its smoky whiff, though nothing burned. I knew it wasn't possible, but the incinerator appeared to be missing the dog, to be commiserating and grieving in deepest silence. I pressed a palm to the warm concrete.

In dusk, in the garden's dead centre, for a strange spell I stood unblinking. Cicadas piped up. Each sounded the same: each was unique.

In the murk between dusk and dark a silhouetted sparrow cut twitchy diagrams like inscrutable equations on a blackboard.

A strange thought introduced itself on the sly – nothing mattered. Nothing mattered now and I could get away with anything; do anything to anybody without repercussion or recrimination. I'd been wronged and now I would do wrong.

Mosquitoes attacked.

In bed I lay frozen. I hadn't done my maths homework again . . . maybe we'd get a day off school . . .

Across the road a sprinkler ticked, hissing every time it turned and every time Leo turned or shifted the top bunk squeaked and trembled.

I heard my voice. "Where do you reckon his spirit went?"

His reply seemed to be forever coming and when it came, the words seemed bent out of shape.

"Who knows."

My torso rose and fell, rose, fell. "What do they do with his body?"

The bunk creaked.

The sprinkler ticked and twitched.

He said, to himself, "How should I know."

I stared at the ceiling.

Through the wall came my sister's sorrowful singing.

Every night she sang herself to sleep. Tonight the song held me frozen, filled me with horror. I wanted to comfort her. Something held me there preventing me. Something had always prevented me.

My stomach tightened.

My sister slept.

My drowsy mind's eye threw up words like pieces of a puzzle come adrift
. . . stone . . . storm . . . soul-bones . . . wishbone soul . . . soul-closing . . .
I stood at the woman's window. My dad shared her bed. In a coffin beside
the bed lay my sister. The dog was nailed to the wall.

I stared unblinking at the dark ceiling.

The flyscreen frame rattled and trembled, chattering. A surge of wind
blew over the house like a bloated, heaving, waterless wave.

Standing at the bedroom window I stared into heaving, sighing, swollen
darkness.

Standing in his nightly spot at the end of the driveway my dad waited
for Gary German.

I wanted to call out to him. I wanted to say something kind – something
simple he could take with him. The wind laid bare his bald patch and I felt
this stab of love. He cupped his palms and tried to get the lighter to work
and gave up and put his hands in his pockets and his hook nose pointed at
the nature strip and he gave the grass a resigned little kick.

German's truck started four doors up the road. My dad whipped his
hands out of his pockets like he'd received an order. German backed out
of his driveway.

I listened to the truck idle a few moments, as if he was looking for
something in his glove box, or tuning his radio. Abruptly the engine
growled.

My dad reached for the passenger door and opened and the sound of a
night-time radio station carried.

try for an UPtown Girrrl,
she's my UPtown Girrrrl,
You know I'm in love with an –

He pulled the door and the truck roared around the corner, all the way
to the next corner at Covering Road, where it turned, roaring with muffled

finality, exiting the neighbourhood.

The wind spoke a secretive, cajoling tongue. Words swirled in my head; words from a dream. Embark . . . Emblazon . . . Embark . . .

I found my shorts in a ball on the carpet.

The flyscreen's clumsy weight and width made me drop it on the carpet with a rattling thwack. Leo stopped snoring. I froze. He rolled over and the bunk rattled. *Wake him, go together. He can throw the stone instead of you. No – go alone. Get back in bed and stay there.*

A gust found its way into the room, brushing my forearm, like a hand.

With my back to the room, like something hatching – something impatient for life – I clamoured and squirmed out of the window. The drop to the flowerbed was no more than a few inches but I misjudged it enough to lose balance.

As I crash-landed in the flowerbed the frame shuddered – a sound that seemed enough to wake the neighbourhood.

Around the front of the car I crept. Hard and knobbly against my soles and toes, the gravel made me picture rosary beads.

In the corner by the front fence, from under the tree with the small green and orange leaves, I chose a white stone the size of an egg.

I tiptoed down the gravel-rosary-beads to the bitumen. *Hail Mary full of grace . . . the Lord is with thee.* On the bitumen I stopped and brushed the pebble-beads from my arches of my soles and the balls of my feet and between my toes.

Now the wind swept me into its current.

The smell of rain rode the wind. The warm bitumen was alive with barefoot nuance.

Ragged clouds scudded so swiftly across the sky the moon appeared to be on a wild voyage in the opposite direction.

A raindrop spattered the road wetting my toes, then another and another. I smelled the dust on the road, I smelled the dust on the road, I smelled the dust on the road. *I have a stone in my hand . . . I have a stone in my hand. I am brave, I am brave . . . I am brave.* I ran with the thing that runs beside us.

Gum trees in gardens rustled rapturous applause. A huddle of baby birds in a crown cried out in a commingling of rising notes. A raindrop hit my tongue and triggered a chant. *Nobody can kill, Huckle-berry Finn, Nobody can kill, Huckle-berry Finn.* My neck prickled. My soles drummed the warm bitumen.

I whipped around in fright at a leaf skating up behind. A heavy wooden gate swung into a wall with a noise like a gunshot. A set of clanging, flailing wind chimes throttled itself.

I ran from the thing that runs behind us.

Ember-orange behind the white blind against her window, hers was the only light burning in her street. The stake quivered in the dark like a tenuous scarecrow. A spindly water metre protruded like a submarine's eye where curb met driveway.

I hurried past telling myself it was only to see the place from a different angle.

Pacing in front of the vacant block, soles burning, I glanced repeatedly at the burning window.

The stone was too much.

The stone was nowhere near enough.

My stiffened claws sweat around the stone. An empty Solo can clattered along the gutter in front of the empty block.

The dark in that vacant block was fuller and thicker than anywhere else. No streetlight cast itself there. No moonlight touched it. A white plastic bag collared on the brambles flapped, like a white flag.

I stared into the block's core transfixed, without knowing, without even suspecting what it was I hoped to see.

I saw the dog standing in the dark; front paw cocked; startled stiff by the sight of me. My skin tingled and prickled from my scalp all the way into my toenails.

He disappeared.

I whispered his name.

I said his name out loud to the dark.

Unblinking, I lobbed the stone in a gentle arc at the spot. The stone was airborne an unreasonable time – as if gravity had suspended.

The stone came back to earth.

The wind lay low a minute before soaring and swinging around with a howl as all the eddying gusto of the night redoubled.

I stepped onto the block's unwelcoming grass and stepped inside a vacuum and searched in circles until I was bamboozled and near sighted and fled.

I came alongside the park, where the gum trees mourned.

Sarah Isaac

Sarah Isaac was born in Wales and lived in Bristol for fourteen years before moving to a remote Scottish glen. She works as an art teacher and has taught in mental health institutions, a secure school and colleges. Now her daughters are adults she finds time to write every day, revising one novel and planning another. The character 'Ada' was created after reading newspapers from the 1870s in Bristol Central Library. A small paragraph told the tale of the daughter of an acrobatic troupe that had been abandoned. The drunken bear came from the same source but was given more words.

The Collector

They wanted danger , my Pa, Dick, Ma, to fall headfirst onto the cobbles, blood running in the gutter. They'd hold their breath when Dick, on Pa's shoulders, swooned in a half circle, when Ma, high in the air, wobbled. They'd sigh with relief when they all landed on their feet, smiling, bowing, curtseying, but you could tell they were disappointed there'd not been an injury.

I liked the tower best, Dick standing on Pa's shoulders, Ma standing on Dick's shoulders, looking across the crowd, leaning forward then back. She'd lift her foot to her mouth, inspecting her toes, all the while the crowd watching, gasping. She'd fold herself in half, turning her body so the top of her head touched Dick's. You could see they were mother and son then, the mirrored heads taking away the things that interfered, facial hair, the gaps in Ma's teeth, the circle of rouge on her cheeks. The men would look as her bosoms fell forward, willing them to fall out of her costume, she said, red and black, stitched up and patched, over and over.

The veins on Pa's arms made ridges you could travel a fingertip against. The humps of muscle in his arms were the shape of Ma's body under the bed clothes. His body told me, told the audience, what this was costing him, his legs braced, eyes tight with concentration.

Dick wasn't as big as my Dad yet, his skin still soft, but not for much longer. They'd have to find someone else if he grew much more, only the money would have to be shared. Still, there'd be more money if they could do more, make it look more dangerous. I heard them, whispering in the night when they thought I was sleeping. The pity of it was, they said, I was of no use.

When they fell to the ground in a whirl of tumbles, my heart would be in my mouth. I should have been collecting then. Dad would fix his eyes on mine. I'd take the cap, remembering to smile and curtsey. Men, smelling of beer, they'd touch me. I'd no padding, no corsets. They'd grab a good handful, fingers in under my skirts if I wasn't quick enough. I never was. Some people would take money out of the cap. I didn't have the words, the strength, to stop them. The audience would go back to the lodging houses, the taverns or further along the street to watch that toothless old bear the Frenchmen had, standing on its hind legs and bleating.

That last time, in North Street, a place full of crowded, mean houses, the Frenchmen weren't there. They'd gone out drinking, leaving the bear chained to the park railings. The peelers arrested them. They'd gone up in front of the magistrate, taking old Bruno with them because the police wouldn't touch him, not the way the fleas were jumping. Ma went to the court. Old Bruno, he lay down in front of the magistrate's clerk. When the magistrate gave sentence Bruno yawned, then broke wind. She said the magistrate didn't even smile when everyone else was laughing. The smell, Ma said, was just terrible. There was a gentlewoman that fainted. The Frenchmen had to leave Bristol, the magistrate said, and not come back because they had failed to supervise their animal. He could have been a menace to the people of Bedminster. That made everyone laugh again. Bruno was too old, drunk, clawless, to be a menace to anyone.

We stood under the eaves of the timbered buildings. I asked Dad for money for bread. He put his hand on my stomach and pushed it, my flesh yielding around his fingers. He said I was greedy, I needed to learn to do without. We stared at the sky and I wished for the clouds to clear and Ma wished to get out of this 'fucking place' and Dad stared at me and the sky with eyes like the thunder that threatened.

The rain fell in great spouts from broken gutters. The Italians that played the music had been complaining, saying it wasn't worth their while. I was no good as a collector. Couldn't Ma and Pa do something about me, make me a look a better, be a bit quicker? They said it in front of me. Everybody has always said everything in front of me. They thought I was stupid. I've learnt, since then. You couldn't live here and be that stupid.

I did the collection, still smiling when thick fingers pinched and prodded. Then I saw Dad's knee give. It was doing that more and more. He had the pole, a poplar trunk, twice his height, lighter than it looked, tied around his waist. Dick was doing a handstand off the top of it. If Pa allowed it to fall forward, if Dick caught it with his hand when he dismounted, it could tear Pa's insides out. His face, just for a second, went still and dark. My brother got ready to dismount, too soon, no showing off up there. The crowd thought it was part of the act. The Italians were good, making the music all dramatic. I should have used that, gone back to those who had given, but I had to stop and watch.

Ma grabbed the cap, darting through the circle, smiling and curtseying. It looked alright, the cap, better than it had for a while. It wasn't enough. Dad shouted, said I should have watched the crowd, smiled more, been quicker, not stopped to pass the time of day with every single one of them. That wasn't fair. I didn't do that. He raised that great red hand of his and walloped me, first one ear, sending my head sideways, making my ear ring, then the other. He always liked to get it regular, just like he put his shoes in a neat pair under the bed every night. I cried. I said I had done my best.

'Your best, Ada' he said, is not good enough.' He hit me again, a punch that would leave the mark of his knuckles on my cheek. He didn't feel the need to make that one equal. My nose was bleeding, the taste of copper in my throat. The Italians shook their heads and packed their instruments away.

I saw her then, Miss Emily. There was a carriage going past and she leant out of the window. Her face looked sad, cross too. Then she was gone and Dad was dragging me by the hair. He gave me some money. He told me to get food and beer, only not like the rubbish I'd got last time or I'd get another hiding. I had to bring it back to the lodgings.

We slept in one room together. I had to shut my ears to the sound of them, the bedframe creaking , the grunt and whimper that meant it was over. Dick snored through it all, through the noises I made when Ma was away, waking long enough to do the act, eat, drink and comb his beginning moustaches.

We weren't meant to bring back food and drink. Mrs Smithson would have a fit if she knew. That's what she made money on. They'd be keeping her talking, Dad telling her tales of when he was in the circus, meeting Mum on the high wire. It wasn't true. Mum was a parlour maid. Dad said she had an unusual sense of balance for someone not born into it. He'd tell Mrs Smithson about what they did to me and Dick when we were babies, holding us to his chest, bringing our legs to his shoulders, twenty times every night, not minding how we cried because that was the only way. It didn't work for me. Sometimes my legs ache for no reason at all.

Dad would do his crab for Mrs Smithson, throwing his arms over his shoulder, landing on his palms, scuttling around the Turkey carpet and I'd sneak up the stairs.

I got some oranges, half price they were, beer, bread and cheese and some change. I thought he'd be pleased. When I got to the lodgings the rain had stopped, sunlight showing the cobwebs clinging to the windowpanes.

I pushed the door open, hearing it catch against the stone floor. Mrs Smithson was in the back parlour. Her hair, lit by the late sun, looked angry. She came out and grabbed my arm really hard and I dropped the beer in the passageway. It spread in a dark pool around my skirts.

'Where are they? ' she said, 'where's that George Butler with his fancy tricks?' She took my basket and looked inside, her mouth tight. 'What's this?' I felt her spittle land on my cheek. 'He keeps me quiet and you sneak up the stairs with this?'

She laughed. It wasn't the kind of laugh people do when things are funny, not like the crowd laughing at Bruno.

'Go on up' she said. 'Go and have a look.'

I could see the masts of sailing ships through the window of our room. There was nothing to hide them, the curtains gone. They were the only decent thing in the room Ma had said, red velvet lined with yellow silk. The beds were bare. The oil lamp with the cracked glass wasn't on the table. Even the picture that had hung above the fireplace, the glass so dark and dingy with smoke you could hardly see the soldiers underneath, wounded and dead, was gone. Our trunk was gone. I looked all around the room, in the big wardrobe, in the chest of drawers. All I found was one dirty handkerchief. It was mine.

Mrs Smithson was standing in the doorway. For a large woman she was light on her feet.

'Seems they forgot about you. Or are you meeting them somewhere?' She started laughing again. 'I think they left you behind on purpose; because you're no use.' She laughed even harder. 'You're no bloody use at all'.

She led me to the door. She wasn't rough. She was still laughing, tears rolling down her fat red cheeks.

I went to the harbour. I found a corner where I could watch the boats and not be seen. I sat there for two days and two nights, only leaving for a drink of water, squatting behind a shed when I needed. I saw sailors with women, grunting and panting, almost next to me. Once I heard a tall black man singing a song not like anything I'd ever heard before. I didn't understand the words. It made me cry.

I didn't see my family. I tried to find the Italians. They'd gone too. I was hungry. I begged but it seemed I was invisible, although I could still see my reflection in the puddles.

The smell from the bakers was so sweet. It was only a loaf of bread. I took it and I ran. I ran straight into a passing constable.

The constable gave me cake and dish of tea. The magistrate sent me to the Girls Reformatory. They wrote about me in the papers, the abandoned daughter of a troupe of acrobats. The girls in the reformatory knew about me. I recognised Miss Emily, remembered her face in the carriage window, her look of sorrow when Dad hit me. She visited, taught fine needlework. 'The girl with the acrobats' she said.

The other girls, they tease me. They've got families that don't want them but there's a difference in leaving and being left behind. They call me Miss Emily's pet. At night, they whisper, their breath hot against my neck.

'Eating treats again?' they say. I pretend I'm sleeping. 'Think we don't know? Greedy bitch.' They pinch and squeeze and tug. I know better than to call out. When their sounds are just a twist of a blanket, the rasp of an uncut toenail against an itch, I sleep.

She's a gentlewomen, Miss Emily, wears fine clothes and her hands, when she holds mine, feel so soft. The way she touches me, just a pat here, a squeeze there, a kiss dropped like a whisper on the back of my neck, there's nothing wrong in it. She says I can be her ladies maid, when I've learnt some proper sewing.

Matron says I should go to Taunton and work in a laundry. There'd be other girls, a decent wage. She doesn't think I'd make a good ladies maid. 'You're too clumsy with the little things' she says, 'and they never seem to last long with Miss Emily, although I'm sure I don't know why.'

Taunton's not on my family's circuit. It's a long way from Bristol. If I work for Miss Emily I'll be in the city. There'll be errands to run. I can look for red velvet cloaks with yellow silk linings. They might be looking for me. It might be my fault, something they told me I forgot or couldn't hear, my ears were ringing so.

I could be a good collector now.

Colter Jackson

Colter Jackson works as a freelance writer and illustrator in New York City and has written scripts for both Tina Fey and UN Secretary General Ban Ki-moon. One of which was funny. She is the author and illustrator of the picture book *Elephants Make Fine Friends*, forthcoming from Penguin in 2015. You can find some of her work in *Tin House, The Rumpus* and *Litro* magazine.

Mountain Goat

Used to be, I could keep a job, keep the lights on, keep the rent paid, keep my hair washed, keep it together in the general sense. I've cleaned hotel rooms, ran a cash register, once I even got on at an insurance office answering and routing phone calls. Lately though – beginning right around the time I turned 28 – I started noticing that when I looked in the mirror I'd see the ghost of my mother and her troublesome habit of losing her mind.

Believe it or not, I have a high school diploma. Even made it through a year of South County Community College before I dropped out and became a full-time fuck-up. To be fair, I was always the girl everyone figured for a criminal or at the very least, a druggie. You hear something enough times, it can feel like the truth.

Walking through the park looking for answers, I encounter an old man and because of the position of the sun behind him, he first appears as a human-shaped hole lumbering toward me. As he draws closer, I see he limps and has acne scarring, but he is beautiful in some important way, in a bone-structure way. He is homeless, I realize and I'm trying not to make eye contact when the man speaks to me.

"God loves you, Mountain Goat. Don't ever forget."

I say, "Hello."

"Hello," he says back. And it's the way he says it that sticks to me, as if he is not conscious of what preceded it. As if God has just spoken through him unbeknownst to him. A familiar hope passes through my body.

By the time we've passed each other, I'm fighting the battle. Any sane person would try to discount the fact that a homeless man has just called them by their childhood nickname. Mountain Goat. It was a name my mother gave to me. People who get desperate can see a sign anywhere, even in a pile of ants or on a piece of toast. But I've been waiting for this. Staggering away, I sit on a nearby bench.

It was the hot end of June, the morning of my 9th birthday. My mother had promised to take me swimming. We lived then in the Ozarks near a man-made lake that made the air thick with the smell of catfish and stink bait. Our bathing suits lived permanently in the glove box. Mine: a modest one-piece I'd chosen. Hers: a pink and black zebra-print bikini. We sped down a country road, gravel crunching under us, dust swirling behind while Kenny Rogers pelted his heartache out of the cassette deck.

She was a good mother so far as I could tell at the time. She was a churchgoer for one thing. She said our congregation was full of whores and gamblers singing of Jesus' blood to the silver sound of tambourines but we went every Sunday. She always split her hamburger in two and handed me the bigger half. When I got in fights at school, she took my side and threatened to beat more than one kid's ass. On the nights she was alone, she'd hold up the quilts on her bed and invite me to sleep beside her. We'd curl up like squirrels, limb upon limb. In church, she whisper-talked to me about which married man had been eyeing her during praise and worship. And on her sad days, she'd beg me to stay home from school and keep her company. "Don't you wanna come get up to no good with me?" I was her co-pilot. Her secret keeper. Her biggest fan. With it always just being the two of us, there was no one else for me to give my love to. Except for the occasional misplaced affection I had for a teacher, she was everything.

The trees reached for us as we blew past and I picked at the duct tape covering a rip in the seat. She said, "You're nine today and being nine I feel that it's time you learn some important things."

I nodded.

"The universe has a language and if you learn to listen, you can communicate with it. I've had messages delivered to me a million different ways. God is one hell of a wiseass, I'll tell you that."

When she spoke, I could see the hole where her tooth was missing. It had been punched out by her own mother way before I was born and she'd swallowed it. I imagined it inside of her, stubborn and undigested.

She pressed on the lighter knob and reached for her cigarette pouch. "He'll tell me things through the TV sometimes, or in cloud patterns. Once I even got a message in one of your shitty diapers. It was the letter P, clear as day. I got on my knees right then and I prayed and he told me to play the lottery."

The lighter popped out and she brought the glowing orange circle to the cigarette waiting in her mouth. "So I played the lottery and I'll be damned if I didn't win fifty bucks. Not a lot of money but back then we were really hurting."

I was looking over at her trembling hands, at the long, lazy lifeline dividing her palm. With no school, the hours were lengthy and spacious for me. My days were punctuated by these swimming trips and I counted on them, the excitement almost painful.

We were about to pull off onto the dirt road that led down to the water where we'd strip down naked to change into our suits, me getting a glimpse of my mother's breasts, puckered like spoiled peaches, my fault, she said because she breast-fed me, but she hit the brakes instead. She reversed into some tall widgeon ditch grass and turned us around. We began to trail a black Pontiac.

"What's wrong? Aren't we going to the lake?" I said, searching her face.

"Not today."

"Why not?"

"God has other plans for us. I had a feeling he wanted to talk to us today."

I looked around for the object that might have indicated that God wanted her attention and I tried hard to keep the doubt out of my voice. "Another sign?"

The December prior, before she'd pulled me out of fourth grade for good in favor of "home schooling," she was supposed to pick me up after the last bell rang. I waited outside until I thought all my fingers were going to fall off. Everyone, even the teachers had gone home. After dark, she rolled up, eyes glassy, hands scuffed and bleeding. God had given her a sign then too. He had shown her an empty house where she could remove the copper pipes. It was easy money if you knew how to find it.

Another sign: a trucker wearing a hat with the number seven walking around Wal-Mart. In the parking lot, she had me hide under a scratchy army blanket in the backseat but I got hot and bored. When I peeked out, the trucker was in the front seat head thrown back, making these noises and I couldn't see my mom but I knew she was there.

Signs came in many forms and delivered all kinds of information. A red bandana could be him showing us how to find some scratch or telling us to eat more vegetables. A dead opossum on the highway could mean it was time to leave town or time to eat supper. Sometimes it was as simple as

God pointing her toward the kind soul that would let her bum her next cigarette. There didn't seem to be much logic to it. God isn't logical, I figured. I tried to see the signs too but they eluded me. I would stare at the water tower or the bumper sticker or the discarded plastic lighter and try to see the message she saw there but I couldn't. She was the only one with the gift. God had chosen her, she told me once.

"How do you know God wants us to follow it?" I asked, defiant for the very first time. "Maybe it means to go home and eat birthday donuts."

"It doesn't."

"Maybe it means to stay away."

"It doesn't. Now quit back talking. What's gotten into you? I know when the Holy Spirit is speaking, Mountain Goat. It would be a sin to ignore it. Remember Jonah?"

Of course. Jonah – the ass wipe. Jonah – commanded by God to go to the sin-ridden city of Nineveh to prophesy. Jonah – who tried to run away by sailing to another town, got tossed overboard, swallowed by a large fish and kept inside for three days. Jonah – brought up when anyone questioned my mother's decision making. I had been learning in Sunday school that God had a round about way of doing things sometimes. Turning people into salt pillars or smiting them with boils, depending on the mood he was in.

We trailed the black car down the dusty gravel, then onto a highway that flattened out before us. The sign this time, according to my mother, was a yellow ribbon tied into a lopsided bow on the tip of the car's antenna. We followed it until I gave up the idea of going back to the lake. With the windows rolled down and the highway wind whipping our hair across our faces, we tailed that ribbon until stars emerged in the darkening sky. This wasn't the first time God had interfered in my day and it certainly wouldn't be the last.

When we'd followed the Pontiac across the state line and I'd drifted in and out of sleep, dreaming of whales and iron anchors and other impossibly large objects, the driver began to slow. He pulled off at a gas station. My mother did the same. A man that reminded me vaguely of a hippopotamus with a long stalactite goatee opened his door and stood stretching. My mom jumped out of the car, barely putting the shifter into park. Feeling a sickness descend over me, I watched from my perch on the center console.

"God told me to follow you."

"Excuse me?"

"I've been tailing you since before you turned onto Highway 65. That ribbon…"

And here she pointed to the pale yellow piece of cloth around the antenna.

"That ribbon made me follow you. Do you have some sort of message for me? I think the Holy Ghost is trying to speak through you."

"Lady, get the fuck away from me."

Mom got up close to his face, right up where she could almost kiss him. I saw her whispering something but I couldn't hear what it was. He shoved her and she went flailing back.

The passenger side door flung open and a fair-haired woman jumped out and went into the gas station and spoke to the attendant. He picked up the phone and I knew where this was going.

At the car, my mother started to pray in tongues. She did this on occasion – not just in church but any time she needed some authority. She lifted her hands over her head and started the chanting that brought so many puzzled stares toward us. The man backed away and even when the fuel gun clicked that his tank was full, he didn't go near my mother. It was almost as if she had some kind of sickness he could catch.

Within minutes a patrol car was there. The policeman shined his flashlight in on me and I smiled up at him. He approached my mother and I heard him saying, "Ma'am, I need you to stop doing that." Mom looked at him and said, "I'm not breaking any law, I have a right to my religion." He looked then at the driver standing nearby watching the spectacle my mother was making of herself and asked if she'd hurt anyone. He looked at her, down on her knees in the gravel, hands reaching up toward heaven, tears streaming down her face and he shook his head. The officer searched the car for booze and drugs and not finding any he looked at me for what seemed like a very long time without saying anything. Then, he let us go.

When we turned around to go home, I could feel my mother's defeat in the car with us like a planet with its own gravity. I felt so small and helpless beside it. I wanted to tell her she wasn't alone against all of it because she had me. But instead, I drew back my arm and hit her across her stomach. The blow landed with a thin slap. She looked at me with a flash of surprised pain but said nothing. I hated myself for doing it and I wished I could take it back but I didn't know how to say sorry. The rest of the drive we were suspended in a cocoon of silence.

She had wanted a sign. So that was what I wanted for her. But even more, I wanted her to hold on to her mind that seemed to be scratching and squirming to get away from her.

A month later, she'd be gone and I'd be in foster care. I tried to believe for a long time that she'd ascended like Enoch. God liked her so much, he'd decided to take her to ride alongside him as he got up to no good. Instead of facing the truth of it, that she'd woken up one morning and left me without ever looking back.

I've wondered a thousand times what the sign could have been that told her to leave. And I've feared a thousand times that there was no sign but that after that day in the car, I'd become like the rest of the world to her. Hopeless. Unbelieving.

Mountain Goat. She'd given me the name because she said I could survive anywhere, no matter how inhospitable the terrain. "The world is cruel, but you are a mountain goat and mountain goats are made for surviving."

I tried to remember this through the roulette of foster care homes – some better than others. But no matter how safe and how clean and how well cared for, there was nothing that could compare to the fearless and intoxicating, albeit dangerous life I had alongside her or fill the mother-shaped hole she'd left in me. The universe became so much bigger than I'd ever known before and it had closed up quietly in her absence like water over a sinking stone.

I know some strange and small part of me has been waiting for the sign that she'd one day send.

I stand from the bench and walk – back toward the beautiful homeless man with the limp, toward the God my mother believed in, toward the God that finally decided to start speaking to me, just today, for the very first time.

I catch up with him sitting against a tree and rustling around in his plastic bags. But when I look closer, I'm shocked to see it's not the man, but my mother. Her clothes are tattered, her face is dirty, hair oily, fingernails framed in black. A cigarette is hanging precariously from her mouth.

"Mountain Goat! My God, where have you been? I've been looking everywhere for you."

Hearing her voice, I fall to my knees and when I touch my face, I'm surprised to find I'm crying.

"Don't cry. Come on. Come give me a squeeze. Let me look at you."

I crawl to her and put my arms around her, she smells like beer and old smoke. I begin to sob telling her how hard it's been since she left, how nothing has ever been right again.

"Oh, billy goat. My little mountain goat. Give me a cigarette, would you?"

I pull back from her and open my eyes but it's not my mother's face I see. Her face and voice are gone as suddenly as they appeared. I'm hugging and crying into the dirty, damp coat of the homeless man. He rubs my back and says, "God loves you, Mountain Goat. That'll always be true."

Danielle McLaughlin

Danielle McLaughlin's stories have appeared in journals such as *The Stinging Fly*, *The Penny Dreadful*, *The Fog Horn*, and in various anthologies, including the 4th Bristol Short Story Prize Anthology. Her awards for short fiction include the William Trevor/Elizabeth Bowen International Short Story Competition 2012, the Willesden Short Story Prize 2013, the Merriman Short Story Competition 2013 in memory of Maeve Binchy, and the Dromineer Literary Festival Short Story Competition 2013. In 2014, she was shortlisted for the Davy Byrnes Award. Her debut collection of short stories is forthcoming from The Stinging Fly Press. She lives in Cork, Ireland.

Beached

When the waters receded, I found a fish in the grass, all dead and glassy-eyed. I picked it up and it came to life, shot right out of my hand. I gave it a name – your name, actually – then watched it thrash and wriggle at my feet until the thrashing and wriggling stopped.

Why am I telling you this? Because if you hadn't left, you could've worked the wire-clippers underwater – those damn useless clippers we bought at Cauldens' Yard – and the calf wouldn't have died. It wouldn't have been swept downriver past the reservoir to end up impaled on the gates of the weir. And yes, I do know it is 4am; such a curious hour in the fields, the animals sleeping, the black lines of ditches like driftwood from some other flood, a flotsam of other, older hurts.

I kept it, that fish with your name, pickled in a mix of lavender water and formaldehyde. I display it on the dresser in the kitchen where anybody who visits can see it, though nobody visits, not even that man from the gun club who used to be so friendly.

It is not my fault that she has woken. Tell her there will be many nights like this: your former lovers calling from wet fields, mouthing, like fish, their silent obscenities as they wait for the next flood.

Keeley Mansfield

Keeley Mansfield has an MA in Writing from Sheffield Hallam University, and was published in the university's anthology, Matter. After graduating, she took a long, unintended break from writing, but returned in earnest in 2013. Since then, she has been longlisted for various prizes including the 2014 Fish Flash Fiction Prize, and will have a story featured in the Autumn 2014 issue of *Wordlegs*. Originally hailing from East London, she currently lives in Dublin, Ireland.

Biscuits for Special Occasions

I've made a picture for Janet and I'm busting to show her. It took me the whole hour of class, and I used up nearly all of our table's blue paint getting the sky just right. Mrs Daniels said it was very good and patted me on the shoulder. Sarah and Bryony were whispering and nudging each other, but I didn't even care; their paintings were both of Bryony's new dog, and they didn't even paint in a background.

It's cold and I left my scarf on the train, so I walk as fast as I can down the Crescent to the house. I never run anywhere. If a new kid asks why, I say I've got asthma and show them my blue inhaler. Or I say I broke my ankle last year and it still hurts. It's true, I did, and it does feel loose sometimes, like it's not attached to the rest of me. Really though, I don't run because I know what I look like, all ugly and sweaty and my face all red, like how my daddy looked when they took him away. I watched the men put him into an ambulance and he looked like he'd been running for hours, he was soaking wet and red as ketchup, but he'd just been screaming, not moving. I need my inhaler when I think about it.

I'm humming a song I heard on the radio and I'm swinging my arms *left, right, left, right* but when I reach the house, something seems wrong. I'd normally hear the little'uns singing and screeching in the garden, or Sandra and Connie would be flying up the road on their bikes, trying

149

to snatch my schoolbag. I wonder whether I've made a mistake and left school too early. It's dark though, so it must be after four; it always gets dark early in winter, and all the lovely lights come twinkling on, and the air smells smoky and delicious. The house looks like a big face with hollowed-out eyes, because there are no lights on in the bedrooms. Usually, all the front windows are blazing yellow, because the kids never remember to switch off the lights or pull the curtains. Sometimes I go round and do it, and then Janet calls me her little caretaker. I like Janet best of all the staff. The others are more interested in smoking fags and drinking coffee that makes their breath stink, but Janet sits with me and looks through my homework or asks me what I did in class. I wonder if she's been round and turned off all the lights to save me the trouble.

I walk up the path towards the front door and something crunches underfoot. At first I think it's a snail; the little'uns scoop them up and fling them at each other. I try and rescue them, because Mr Everett told me they're really important in the food chain. I'm part of the food chain too, but I'm at the top. I'm definitely above Sarah and Bryony. I take another step, *crunch*. I can't see what it is because the security light hasn't come on, so I crouch down and feel around with my fingers. Something sharp catches me – can snails bite? But no, I rub my fingers together carefully and it's glass. Loads of it, big pieces and tiny shards and splinters. The last time there was broken glass, it was one of the older boys, Jerry, flinging a beer bottle at Patrick. Patrick was trying to confiscate the beer, because Jerry's not supposed to drink in the house, and Jerry got really angry and threw the bottle. It missed Patrick, hit the wall and exploded into hundreds of pieces. Patrick balled up his fists and stood very still, because the staff aren't allowed to touch the kids. Jerry ran up to his room and we all came out from where we were hiding to see the mess. The beery smell was disgusting but the green glass was so pretty against the boring old beige carpet tiles.

Mrs Daniels says I have a good eye for colour.

I walk along the path to the front door, *crunch crunch crunch*, and press the bell. No one answers. I wish they'd give us keys, but they can't risk any of the kids losing them. The house is supposed to be completely secure, because some of the kids have parents who want to steal them. I wish my daddy would come and steal me, but he's in the hospital and they lock all the doors there. Jerry said my daddy's a raving lunatic but he's not, *he's not!* and I've told Jerry that if he says it again, I'll tell the staff about the drink he's got hidden in his room. He said he didn't care, but he's not mentioned anything about daddy since then. I put my hand against the glass door to look through, and the door creaks open. I walk in and stand at the bottom of the stairs...but what if it's a trick, and they're all waiting to jump out at me? They've done it before, the little'uns and some of the older ones too, jumping out as I was coming in from the kitchen with a bowl of custard. I dropped the bowl, and peed myself a little bit too, though none of the kids knew that. I was so upset about the custard, because there wasn't enough left for another portion.

Usually Ray or Susie would have given themselves away by now, because they'd giggle or trip over their own feet, but there's not even a sniffle. I listen carefully, because you never know what might be coming for you, or what clues you might miss. I can only hear my own breathing and the *badump-badump* of my heart. Nothing happens when I flick the light switch on and off, on and off. Perhaps there's been an accident and the wires have come down outside. It happened once after a storm, when a tree came down and snapped a cable. The men from the council couldn't come and fix it until the next day, so we all sat together in the living room with torches. Janet sent Connie down to the corner shop for biscuits and sweets, and we sat around eating them and making up stories until everyone started to fall asleep. Janet gave each of us a hug when it was time to go to bed, and anyone who was frightened could sleep in the living room with her. It's the best night I've had since I first came here. I don't remember many of the others, which Janet tells me is because I block things out, but I remember that night without the electricity like it was yesterday. I ate half a packet of chocolate marshmallows and felt really sick, but it was a nice sick, if you know what I mean.

The curtains are still open and the street lamps and the big cheesy slice of moon are giving me a bit of light to see. I take a few deep breaths and for the first time I notice a strong smell. It's a damp, burning smell, like the time the older ones had a barbecue in the back garden and it got out of control, and they threw water over it to put out the flames. The smell stings my nose. I look in the living room and the kitchen, and the family room too. (It's a funny name for a room, because there's never been a family in there, as far as I know.) I'm getting used to the smell now, but I can't find anyone. Jerry should be watching telly, Sandra and Connie should be arguing, and Susie should be at the kitchen table, drawing a picture with the tip of her tongue stuck out. My stomach feels bad, like I really need to eat something. I push a chair against the worktop in the kitchen, climb up to the top cupboard and grab a packet of biscuits. We're not allowed to help ourselves, but only the moon can see me. I step down from the chair and that old moon-face makes my shadow fall across the room, so that I look like a fat giant. *He's on to me!* I feel wheezy so I take a couple of puffs from my inhaler and breathe out slowly. My breath sounds wrong, as if I'm standing in an empty swimming pool. A cloud comes to my rescue then and covers the moon's eyes. I bite into a biscuit, crunch. Ginger nuts. They're only brought out for special occasions, but this feels like a special occasion so I eat another one. I pull the kitchen curtains and chew in the dark.

I need to decide what to do, and *plot my next move*. We learnt about *plotting* in English last week when we were writing stories. You can't have a story without a plot, says Mr Abraham. I don't like this story's plot, so far, but Mr Abraham says you can always change the plot to make a story better if you're the one in charge. I want to be in charge of all my stories. I want my story to be: I work as hard as I can, pass all my exams and get out of this place, and then find a good job and earn lots of money. Then maybe I can buy a house for me and daddy, and maybe we could even get a dog. A better dog than Bryony's. We had one when I was little, but it got run over, and daddy was so upset he said he'd never have another one. I'm sure I could change his mind. He cried a lot though and made terrible moaning sounds in the night that made me think there was a ghost in the house. But I mustn't think about that, not about ghosts or dead dogs, because the house is dark and I'm scared enough already, and I might pee myself if I get really, really frightened. And then if this is all a trick, I'll smell of pee and I'll never live it down.

I leave the house, pulling the door shut behind me, and I walk quickly back along the Crescent up to the train station. If everyone has gone away and there's no one to look after me, I'll go to the hospital and stay with daddy. I know it's in Upminster; once I get there, I can ask for directions. There's a breeze picking up now, sending crisp packets and drink cartons dancing along the platform. The big clock hanging over the *Next Train Approaching* sign says 4:57pm.

The train pulls in, *takka-takka takka-takka*, the brakes hiss and the doors whoosh apart. There are no free seats so I stand with my back against the door on the opposite side, and reach into my bag for a biscuit. If I eat one at every stop, I should be able to make them last for the whole journey. I mustn't let anyone see the packet, and I mustn't drop any crumbs. I'm always setting myself rules – Janet calls it my *coping mechanism*. Janet seems to have a name for everything, and sometimes I don't understand what she means, though I pretend I do.

A woman gets on and stands very close to me. She is wearing a thin blouse that shows her bra, and hoops on her ears big enough for a tiger to jump through. She catches me looking at her, and she stares back at me until I feel squirmy. For something to do, I decide to break a rule, pull out the packet of biscuits and offer her one. She looks at me for a bit longer – me in my school uniform and my hair in plaits and my plastic glasses halfway down my nose on account of it being so warm on the train – and then she smiles without showing her teeth and takes a biscuit.

"Thanks! I'm starving. Missed lunch."

"Take another one if you want?" I can smell her perfume, it's fruity. Oranges. I have a flash of being in a garden on a woman's lap with the sun shining into my face, and then it's gone.

"No thanks, mustn't ruin my dinner." I hadn't thought about dinner. What time do hospitals serve dinner? What does daddy eat? *What if these biscuits are all I'll have?* I tuck the packet back into my bag and silently promise not to eat any more until I get to Upminster. I'm breaking another rule, but I'm in charge. I wait until the woman has finished eating before speaking again.

"Are you on your way home from work?"

"Yes, I work in Stratford. Do you know where that is?"

I only know the streets around the house and my school, but I don't want her to think I'm stupid so I nod. She points at the tube map above us.

"My stop's Upminster Bridge, second to last. How about you? You're travelling quite late to be only getting home from school now, aren't you?"

"I'm going to Upminster to visit my daddy."

"That's a long journey for you, I'm surprised you travel all that way by yourself. Doesn't your mother worry?" She's looking at me suspiciously now and my face feels hot.

"I don't have one."

"Oh. Well, why doesn't your daddy come and collect you?"

I don't like these questions so I keep my mouth clamped shut and when the doors open on the other side of the carriage at Plaistow, I turn and push through all the people and tread on someone's foot and don't even apologise, and I Mind the Gap and walk quickly down to the end of the platform.

I watch the train pull away, and there are people's faces squashed against the windows, some sleeping or nodding their heads to music. The clock on the platform says 6:05pm so it must be broken, but it's definitely getting late, because there aren't many people about, and I'm starting to feel very hungry. If today was a normal day, I'd be sitting in my red jumper and my jeans with the ripped knee, and I'd be eating Shepherd's Pie because it's Thursday, with tinned pears and custard for afters. And I'd be helping Susie with her spoon because she has trouble holding it properly. Then I'd show Janet the painting I made her, and she'd tell me I was a good girl and maybe she'd even give me a hug like she did the night we had no electricity. To stop my eyes watering, I focus on the lights, which are nice and bright on the platform.

When the next train to Upminster pulls in, it's half-empty, and just seeing the orange seats and the posters for holidays and chocolate bars makes me feel better. I'm sitting down when I see a policeman get on. Could the woman on the other train have phoned him and reported me as a runaway? He's seen me and he's coming towards me, so I jump up and manage to get off the train before the doors close, but he's right behind me, and then I'm running along the platform. As I go, I think, *I'm running, I'm actually running!* And then I'm not running anymore because my ankle has turned over and I'm on the ground, and my face is stinging and my bag has turned upside down and emptied itself out, and the biscuits are everywhere and the painting I did for Janet is in a puddle and it's ruined. Then the policeman is crouching beside me and asking, *are you Amy Bannon?* I say I am, and he says,

"That's good, because we've been getting worried about you."

He helps me up and leads me to a green bench on the platform, and I've grazed my knees and my cheek is throbbing. The policeman takes a clean tissue out of his pocket and hands it to me, and I wipe the blood off my knees and dab my cheek while he explains that there was a fire in one of the bedrooms, and it spread along the corridor, and everyone had to be evacuated.

"What about the glass outside?"

"The firemen smashed the windows to rescue some of your friends from the rooms upstairs."

They're not my friends, I want to say. They're just the kids I live with. He must think I look worried, because he adds,

"Everyone is safe and sound."

"And why were there no lights on?" "You're a curious little girl, aren't you. The electricity is off as a *precaution*. Do you know what that means?" I nod, even though I'm not sure. He takes the mucky tissue away from me and gives me a clean one. He has long, brown fingers and big fingernails with ridges across them. I wonder whether his hands are cold, and whether policemen are allowed to wear knitted gloves. He's making notes on a small pad with a pencil.

"So you went back to the house, and there was no one there at all? A member of staff, Janet, was supposed to stay and wait for you."

"She wasn't there," I say, and he frowns.

"Perhaps there was a *miscommunication*, and she went back to your school to fetch you instead. But here you are, riding the Tube so late on your own."

"Please don't tell my daddy," is all I say, and the policeman shakes his head and says he won't, of course he won't. He scribbles another note on his pad.

When the train to Edgeware Road *takka-takkas* into the station, the policeman places his long fingers on my shoulders and guides me onto the train. He's taking me to the hostel where the other kids are staying for the night. He gives me my bag and the biscuits that didn't fall out of the packet, and I don't mention that my painting is still in the puddle. I think about the paint colouring the rainwater, the blue leaking out of the sky, the brown from Janet's hair, the green from daddy's shirt, the one he was wearing when I last saw him. I offer the policeman a biscuit, but he smiles at me with all his teeth and shakes his head and says, no Amy, you have them. And so I do, one after the other until they've all gone.

Fiona Mitchell

Fiona Mitchell is the author of *The Maid's Room* which was shortlisted into the final three of the 2013 Wow Factor Debut Novel Competition run by literary consultancy Cornerstones. That same year, one of her short stories was commended in the Yeovil Prize. She has almost completed the first draft of her second novel, despite getting distracted by writing short stories. She lives in London where she works as a freelance writer focusing on interiors, health and true life stories. @FionaMoMitchell

The Colour of Mud

I am never gonna be clean, even though I wipe myself down seventeen times a night. It's the mud, see.

I pull my scarf around my face and jump puddles alongside the wall of trucks, grey ones, black ones, all blanketed by the dirt.

There are three men playing poker at a table they've set up in the middle of the drag. A standing man, his leg bent up on a chair, blows a tuneless harmonica. A jar on a table beside him is scabbed with ash.

I step forward and the mud sucks my leg down knee-deep. I grunt and slurp it out.

The lights of a bar flash on and off: *The Good Times Saloon*, the scaffolding on the roof a kind of skeleton. An open kitchen fogs oil and fried plantain. Further up the drag, the cooking mixes with the night stench. Petrol, tobacco, skin slicked in sweat.

There are echoes of laughter and the underfoot beat from a song on the radio.

I pass an island of scorched grass and stare down searching for remarkable signs of green. There's no such thing as colour in this non-existent town. It's not on no map, but the truckers know just where it is, halfway along the Western stretch of the Nakuru-Eldoret highway.

I step forward and, splat, the mud rises and swells between my toes. One of the sisters told me people in other places pay good money to cover themselves in mud. Beneficial for the skin or some such nonsense. But me, I'd pay good money not to have it coating my calves, my hair. It's a smelly kind of chocolate, that's what I tell myself anyhow.

I nod at the bartender who comes out of The Chicago and sets two bottles of beer on the wood.

I step into an alleyway. People brush against my shoulders as they pass; they're too busy trying not to breathe in the fat air to catch my eye.

A roach scuttles up the wood, its antennae level with my mouth and something tickles me there and I slap and rub and some other critter loses its life on my face.

I heave my feet through the mud and plunge them down, flinging spots on to my dress. I don't need many different clothes. The mud makes new patterns every day, see. I'm a regular model for its designs. An arc of teardrops, a polka dot spray, a hot air balloon to carry me far above the slums and their rickety roofs, above the lorries. Above the dogs, ears back, teeth bared, throats gargling. Above the bars and the faded crisp wrappers blowing in circles across the wet.

Them clothes designs are always the same colour: The bark of a tree, the depths of a latrine, dried blood. Who knew brown came in so many shades?

I walk on through the shed-lined alleyway, my eyes on the rectangle of light at the end. A dozy buffalo has lost its direction and bumps against one wall, then the other. I smack its backside and it trundles faster now.

There are no numbers on our places, but you can tell who's in them tonight anyhow. A plank peeling once blue gloss and a mound of spongy cigarette stubs on the ground, that's Susan's place. Further down, the one with the mat outside and the wellington boots, that's Hildah's. Us sisters always trying to add a bit of bright here and there, but the elements win, painting everything the colour of mud.

One of the women is coming towards me. *The Rescuers*, that's what we call them. This one's Esther, the ginger wig tipped slightly on her head so that her own baby tufts show through.

She smiles, her teeth grouted with dough. I think of Sandra saying that she's hungry. She goes to school now where there's enough rice and then some. When I'm working, like now, one of the sisters looks after her with the other kids. Tonight, it's Bimdogo's turn. She will be pacing the floor, armed with a folded newspaper ready to swat the constant insect intruders.

'Hey! You in a hurry?' shouts Esther when I'm way past.

I turn and sidle back to her. The air is so swollen in this tunnel you could squash it between your fingers.

'Gonna be a busy night,' I say.

'I seen all the lorries,' goes Esther. 'More than usual.'

She coils her arm tighter around the basket and I look inside. It's like waking up, seeing that confection of squares on the weave. Purple ones, red ones, green ones. All covered with loops and letters. *Sure*: five hundred times over. The words glisten in the glare of the bulb drooping from a high wire.

'Come on, don't be shy,' goes Esther.

I dig in and scoop a handful.

'Thanks,' I say and on I walk.

Something scurries past, fur stroking my shin. I count five of them and then they're gone. Like I say, I am never gonna be clean. But nothing round here is either, so I fit right in.

Besides I'm lucky aren't I? It's not like they are bad men who come to me all hours. One or two leave without paying. And rumours fly. The girl strangled in her bed. The woman punched until her eye purpled. But it's never happened to me. And it never will.

Here it is, my place for tonight. The corrugated iron lopsided on the roof, the mottled Perspex square with the curtain that used to be turquoise until the sun drank up the dye.

And who's outside, but Julius? He's a regular, Julius. Every second week.

I flick my head, pull back the curtain and he follows me in. It isn't much, but it's mine for the next long hours. There's a basin in the corner to collect the rain. A shelf on one side, with a cup on top and a pile of folded cloths. And then there's the stairs slicing their way down the middle. But I never take customers up there. Up there is mud free and men free. It's the nearest I got to clean in this nowhere place.

Julius smiles and shrugs and sits down on the bench. I sit beside him and he takes my hand for the count of fifty. He closes his eyes and imagines. Just like the other men, Julius is away from home, for up to eight weeks, sometimes longer, without seeing wives, without seeing little ones. So I don't say much and let him pretend. I peel my dress down, take the fat fingers and cup them where I think they want to go.

The time is right pretty much straight away so I pull at his zip, take one of the squares from my pocket and climb on top of him. I rock for a while and then it's done.

I take the note that he pushes into my hand and hope that he don't open his eyes as I pull up the dress and wipe myself down with the cloth.

He doesn't go straight away, see. He sits on, quietly at first, biting a lip, examining a fingernail.

It sits heavy in his silvery face, that I might be his daughter, his wife, if something were to happen to him. He feels so sorry for me that I get to feeling bad for him and I give a gentle punch to his shoulder.

'Come on, brother,' I say.

And he nods and I think, *Don't go crying on me now.*

And he goes on nodding and when he looks up, his eyes are yellow from the light stewing through the Perspex and I smile so hard at him that he smiles right back.

He takes me by the shoulders and says, 'Thank you, Dolly.'

And I am glad that none of them know my name.

'Next time,' Julius says and the curtain falls closed behind him.

I smooth out the sheet, thinking that I really must wash it, but then there'd be just the bare wood while it dried. And the bench would get dirtier still.

'Excuse me,' a voice calls, but I don't answer.

'Excuse me,' the voice goes again.

I roll my eyes, make a kissing sound with my mouth and pull back the curtain.

He's not like the others, the man standing there. If I could call him a man. He is younger than the rest. And that, I'm about to learn, isn't the only thing that's different about him.

'You got money?' I go.

'How much?' he replies.

'Three hundred,' I go.

He nods, eyes going left to right in the alleyway though I don't know what he's worried about. There's only me and the sisters and the men they're working, see.

My eyes fix on that porcelain cheek with its tight, closed pores. *Just a boy*, I think and stop myself from shaking my head or raising my eyes to the ceiling again. After all, there's nothing there I want to look at, save a triangle of mould and a cobweb I've been meaning to brush away.

The boy sits on the bench, not doing, not saying nothing.

I stand over him.

I walk over and kneel in front, reach my hand towards the zipper.

His hand goes on top of mine, it stays there.

'Don't,' he goes.

'Boy, why you here?'

'Same as the rest,' he says.

This time he lets me undo the zipper. I tear open a square and climb on top. It don't take long for him to respond.

But no, he's not like the others. He keeps his eyes open for starters. His breath smells of yellow tea, a flavour I hate. And I jerk my head away as he leans towards me with that doughy look in his eyes.

It is over, fast.

'Sorry,' he goes.

I smack my hand to my still naked chest and laugh heartily.

But then his face goes slack and he's looking into me.

I loop the straps of my dress over my arms and throw the cloth into the corner of the room like it never even happened.

'Don't be staring with those dog eyes,' I say. And, there I go again with the pity tap.

They've all got their stories and for a moment he don't need no words to speak his.

'You OK?' I ask.

He nods.

'What's your name?' I venture even though I know it'll be a lie that leaves his lips.

'Kanji,' he says, still taking me in, dead-on.

The curtain doesn't quite reach the ground but there's no feet, no flip-flops, no boots waiting to come in.

'Bet your mama pleased you got a job,' I go.

He shakes his head and stands.

'Sorry Ma'am,' he says.

I laugh through my teeth. It's years since anyone called me that. Mama, yes, but Ma'am? He must be about seventeen, this boy.

The room has cast a shadow over half his face, a face like it's been moulded from clay. The ears are small, pressed flat against his head. His two front teeth are angled all wrong and those eyes, they are tin, copper, tea – all the colours of the mud in the changing light.

'You're on your way to... ?' I ask.

'Just passing through. First time on the road.'

'First of many, I guess.'

'Taking tea,' he goes.

He folds his arms and carries on staring.

I should have washed that sheet with its clouds and its wrinkles, but what's the point when it dirties again after an hour or so.

'You should go,' I say. 'I got customers. At least, I will have.'

'How can you do what you do?' he asks.

I laugh again, slapping my thigh.

'It's obvious, isn't it?' I shriek.

I hold out my hand, rubbing my thumb and fingers together, but still he don't get it.

'Why?' he goes, that forehead folding.

'Boy,' I say. 'I got customers.'

He takes the note from his pocket, flattens it out in the air, so that it makes the sound of a cat's cradle rebounding across Sandra's tight fingers.

It is a big note, too big. My hands remain rooted in my pockets. I'm not no thief.

'It's not that much,' I say.

'No, I...,' he shakes his head.

'You sure?' I go.

And he shrugs so I reach out my hand. He shuffles slowly towards the curtain and I turn away then, shutting the note in my fingers.

When the curtain closes I get on to my knees – more mud – and pull a rusty box from its place in the floor. I push the note in. Better give it to the school tomorrow morning, stop anyone being tempted.

'Ahem.' Someone clears their throat outside, a shadow in the slit.

I pick up the sheet, turn it the other way, clear imaginary dust motes from my dress, check the corners of my mouth for crust.

I pull back the curtain.

'Hello Dolly,' the man goes. I don't recognise him at first. It's been a while.

He takes off his trousers and sits limply on the bench, a pillow of skin hanging low. I take a long, slow breath. He'll take ages, I remember him now. I don't always remember their faces, but each one got their own smell. And, this one got the halitosis.

A production line, that's what this is. I do the same thing for each one. No contact above the neck. And no kissing. And always a rubber. It just takes one after all. I was sloppy a few years back, but seeing Monica with that slow puncture, her fat being stripped away, well, I don't need another reminder. Most of the sisters don't up the ante. We got an agreement, see. Keep it clean. As clean as it can be with the mud and the latrines which belch their stink.

Afterwards, this one hands me the bog standard three hundred shillings.

I whip back the curtain but there's no one else out there. Laughter from a stall. I pull the damp pants off and push them into my pocket. I take the alleyway and dry off.

I walk past the men with their froth moustaches and roll-your-owns. One of them caterwauls and another nods my way. Two cattle, bells ringing, stumble past. I stab my earrings through the holes and go inside the Tawakal bar. I dilly-dally towards the counter, playing with my coins. And then a man steps from the shadows at the side.

'I got this,' he goes, handing some money to the barman.

He has a pointed chin, a hooked nose. It is a face of sharp angles.

I swallow the beer. He downs his and orders another. And then I get to pretending, touching the bottle to my lips every now and then while his eyes scan me head to muddy toe.

Another girl walks in, a white beanie on, a grey skirt and stands there, hand on hip. I pass her the half empty bottle.

'Asante,' she goes.

I follow the man outside, through the boot-sucking dirt, to a sign which says *Lodging*. We pass doors, some with graffiti on them, others with scratches, some open, some closed. His key rattles the lock. The fluorescence is headache bright.

He don't waste time, trousers whispering. I pull down the top of my dress and show him what I got, point the square in his direction.

He sneers. 'I don't do that,' he goes.

'Well, if you don't, I don't,' I reply, looping a strap back on.

'You owe me now,' he shoots back.

I fold my arms. The door is off-white between the triangle of his legs.

'What?' I snap.

'The beer,' he goes.

I take a step to go round him and he catches my arm.

'My way,' he says, tugging at my dress.

I try to pull the other strap on to no avail.

Then he twists me round, marches me and presses my face to the mosquito-patched wall.

His zipper scrapes.

'I've got the HIV,' I say.

His elbow comes away from my back.

'You're bluffing,' he goes.

I unglue my cheek from the wall.

I pull my dress up to reveal my thigh and there it is, the circle of raw skin beaded with scales.

He looks at the impressive scar and his shoulders ripple. I stand tall, puff my chest and before I head past him towards the door, I wince at his open fly.

I work the handle, then I'm gone.

Back in the bar, I buy a drink. Ginger beer. A can with a straw. It doesn't take long to get picked up. This time, we go to the Paradise.

'I won't do it with the door closed,' I tell him.

He tears open the square. Over his shoulder, I see a man in a hooded top peeking through the crack.

When I leave, the man in the hoody taps me on the arm. I go with him to the Eagle's Nest. I don't get no more trouble.

Later, the sun balloons in the sky. Black dots skitter the air. Someone coughs and can't stop coughing.

A woman with plaits down either side of her head yawns, her arms stretching wings. Crickets hum a morning celebration.

One of the rescuers gives a one-armed hug to a girl with a leopard skin scarf around her neck.

Another rescuer has set up a table with a big silver urn. She offers a steaming cup to a young one, sixteen at most.

I take one of the hot tin cups and a piece of bread from the table and walk on, past the discarded milky balloons, the beer bottles abandoned in the dirt. I turn down the alleyway, past the wheezing snores coming from a slum. The money in my pants welts into my pelvis and on I walk. Then I go inside, climb the stairs, glancing at the cup with each cautious step. The engines roar their departure.

I sit down, raise my hem, then set the burning cup on top of the scar on my thigh. The too-hot tin works a treat. The tea is watery, amber. I don't drink it, but leave it there on my skin as it goes slowly cold. After a while, the scar is fresh again, crimson.

I tip the tea down my throat then.

I put the empty cup on the table as I pass and take sucking steps along the highway, blank now except for the churned mud and the tyre tracks.

I walk and walk, and sing. 'I won't care 'cause you see I'll be gone.'

A grey heron soars overhead.

And then there's grass, lots of it. The colourless, nameless place seems further away than it is.

I'm here at the line of wooden huts. A woman sits outside one of them, a purple scarf wrapped close around her head, her face scribbled with lines. A naked child runs, its bare bottom dimpling and catching the sun. I take a bite of my bread and smile at the woman. She doesn't smile back but closes her eyes in gentle recognition.

Inside the hut, chalked with an outside flower, Sandra is on the floor, swaying one of the younger ones in her arms. She looks up as I fight with the door.

'Mama,' she says.

She pushes the little one on to the mat beside her and gets up. She is in my arms. Her hair has its own smell. Passion fruit. Vanilla. And she shines me a smile and I catch it and hold it right here in my chest.

I push some notes towards Bimdogo, but she shakes her head.

'Tonight, we swap,' she goes.

And I nod, the thought of it flaring in my stomach. Because tonight there will be no beer, no jabbing, no lies.

Tonight there will be fat cheeks and the soft breath of sleeping children.

Tonight the mud will be sugar dry and the lorries faraway.

I push a hibiscus into Sandra's hair, her nose shiny. Her mouth fumbles with that wobbly tooth.

'Your fang,' I go. 'Let Mama try.'

Sandra pushes the tooth forward over her lip.

But I must wash first.

We walk a long way, Sandra and me. Past the cloud of flies over the open ditch, an old newspaper fanning beside it; past a woman with a child strapped in canvas across her front, legs dangling. We walk past a man, a branch of thorn melon in his hand.

There's only a single person in front of me at the tap at this hour, filling a plastic bottle with the gush.

She gives me a mock salute as she passes and then I'm on my knees, letting the water rain down on my hands. I splash it into my face and gasp. Then I turn around and thank God no one else is queuing. The water is a shock between my legs.

And then I'm clean and me again.

We head back to the shack and along the way, the mud is just right for dirt circles. I draw one around us and laugh.

'Come on, Mama, come on,' Sandra insists.

But though she pulls on my arm and leans, I don't step outside the line. Then, just as her face twists with the force of pulling, I stumble and fall backwards in a burst of dust.

'Your turn,' she shouts. 'Your turn to pull me.'

One week later and it's my turn again. The circle on my thigh is fading so I start the night by buying tea from the Tawakal. I set it to work and it comes up redder than I hoped. *It will be a good night*, I think. And I am right.

The third man I take, he don't want to open the square, but I show him the welt and he pushes it on reluctantly. He gives up halfway through.

'Put me off,' he says, flicking his hand towards my leg, his mouth turned down at either side.

He pays me the shillings anyhow and off he goes, his trousers and his shoulders sagging.

I wait a while and just when it looks like I'll have to go hunting at the bars, footsteps slap up the tunnel.

'Hello again,' he says.

I know it begins with a K. I just can't remember how it ends.

It is streamlined and quick, just like the last time. He still smells of yellow tea. He still looks young and he still keeps his eyes open.

He pulls the notes from his pocket and sets them on the bench. I turn away. There is a small thunk and then he is gone.

I sit down on the bench and look at the peach that he's laid there. It lights up the scene. I turn it velvet in my hand and the newspapers, stuck to the wall, fade out and all I can see is pink. Pink and a slash of yellow.

The next few nights are painted with colour. Then the peach goes wrinkly and grows a circle of badness. I bite that and spit it away.

I walk from that nameless place back to the compound with its chalked walls, with the sunshine smiles of children, with the wheel-less bike leaning against the Acacia tree.

Sandra bites into the peach, the sweetness trickling gold down her wrist.

It's only then that I see her school book is open and the juice has pooled over the pencil grey letters on the page.

Emma Murray

Emma Murray is a writer and tutor. Having grown up in rural Oxfordshire, she now lives in North London, where she tutors children and young adults in literacy, encouraging them in their creative writing and reading skills. Emma studied English Literature at Cambridge, and then Script Writing at Goldsmiths, where she gained a distinction for her MA feature script. She has written several short stories, recently completed her first novel and is currently working on a second.

Tethered

I come here to watch the sun rise. Today, I've bought Luke with me. You are in the Senate room, deciding our future, and so Luke must be my messenger. We press our faces to the glass and gaze out into the darkness. I feel Luke get fidgety next to me, and then grow suddenly still. His young eyes have seen the first rays of sun. Light creeps slowly around the side of the earth below us. Soon I see it too. The tethers appear slowly in ghostly silhouette, those nearest first, like trailing limbs, then the rest steal into view; a hundred thousand tentacles reaching up from the cloud-swept Earth. Our stations float above them, lumbering and slow; mechanical whales in a deep, black sea. Directly below us, our tether falls away; an anchor down to Earth.

Every night now, I dream of the owls. I make tea and I think of the caretaker sipping from our china cups. I wash and clean my teeth and I'm washing off the thick soot, rubbing it from my gums. I cough, as I'm afraid I do often now, and it's my mother. Her eyes stream, her face is smeared black. She's laughing. And then she sees the owl. Or owls, I should say. I know that you know this story but I feel I have nothing else left to give. I think now that this is the greatest memory I possess. I hope I can make you understand.

When we first came up the Tethers I was carrying you in my belly. We were like the Pilgrim Fathers, escaping to a new, better world. Not everyone could come of course, but all I knew was that I was getting you out. We would be safe. You might never see real grass or blue sky or a horse or pigs in a farmyard, as I had when I was a girl, but you would never grow sick from infected water. You would never feel the acid rain on your hair. Your eyes would not grow red; your lungs would not get clogged with smoke. You would survive; would thrive even. Comparatively.

It must seem strange to you now, that we never thought beyond a decade or so. But you never saw the Earth as it was. When I stepped into that lift with you safe inside me, I felt only complete relief. The struggle was over. I did not want to fear a seemingly distant future.

The day of the owls, I'm in the old farm kitchen, playing the piano. I'm seven. Mum is washing carrots to make soup. They're lush and orange, still muddy from the earth. They have irregular, knobbly shapes; the kind rarely seen now.

The sun is streaming in through the big sash windows. It seems doubly bright as the patio and garden outside are still wet and dripping from the storm. The heat of the cities would create fronts. Aggressive electrical storms would start over London and move south into Devon. Devon was one of the last rural strongholds. The storms could last for days. I'd stood by the window that morning as it finally grew light and watched the rain sluice down, like God was pouring it out of a huge, divine bucket.

Mum's been going mad at the useless builder. He's meant to be sealing the windows – its basic regulations and our old farmhouse must be made to comply. But he left in the afternoon, complaining about fluttering sounds in the chimney. Now, as Mum chops her carrots, and I struggle to decipher the complex arrangements of notes on the stave, base clef for the left *and* right hand, we hear it too.

Father told me stories of how, after the first storms, they'd gone out to find the earth strewn with the stiff, electrocuted bodies of birds and animals. But no one has seen a wild animal for years.

We approach the fireplace and look up. About a foot into the chimney's shaft is a closed flap, shutting off the upper parts. My father made this flap in the summer, after he began to fear wisps of travelling smog from London. Father kept up to date with the debates and advances with something like a religious fervour, though he understood little of it. I think he was truly terrified. But the world had been about to end for as long as I'd been alive, and I paid little attention. I know you will understand this. We are all now children of the apocalypse.

I think we thought that, as they had made the Tethers, they would make something else, the next, hopefully ultimate, solution. The Tethers themselves took years to be born. When we first heard about this material strong and light enough to build into space, it was just one of many proposals. A company that built skyscrapers said that astronauts had been living quite comfortably for years out in space stations. Why not the rest of us? The first tether snapped a week after completion. The ten construction men inside were popped out into space. The next tether was four years away. But when it arrived, it wasn't one but forty, thin, wavering arms stretching up into space; vertical passageways to safety. The next year another ten thousand were built.

I remember thinking that if we were out of the way, perhaps the earth would have time to rest; that perhaps one day we could move back. I know you will laugh to hear me say such things. You cannot tell me what goes on in that Senate room, but I hear the rumours of exhaustion, of stockpiling. In the canteens, they say the earth is all but dead, that cast off is our only hope. You will say it's not true. But I see the grey tiredness in your eyes. It matches my own. We all know what this vote is for.

Mum calls the caretaker. He comes gruffly up the garden path with his stick. He's an old man, past retirement age. His arthritis gets worse almost by the day now. Mum says he won't work for us much longer. His stick is between a rake, a hoe and staff, so that as he stumps crossly along, using it as a prop to help him walk, he looks something of an agricultural wizard.

You've never seen a field, have you my love? I'm so sorry for that. I wish I could show you the paddock that ran around our house, the oak trees in the south east corner, long dead of course, but still beautiful. I'm sorry that I took it all so for granted. I thought I wanted to go to London. We could see it on the horizon, huge and grey, the air around it always heaving with the interminable rain. When I went there of course I realised it was Hell, but by that time there was no Devon left to return to.

The caretaker sips his tea and looks critically at the chimney and Father's flap. The fluttering becomes more agitated. "Could be jackdaws," he says. "Or squirrels, taking shelter in yer chimney. Last night's storm was a big'un," but I can see he doesn't believe it.

Mum has prepared Father's tools, and the caretaker goes to work on getting the flap open. Mum and I watch. Father's technique, whilst thorough, is not orthodox. Spurred on by half-understood fears, he's fixed more than thirty nails in place at centimetre gaps, and covered the whole contraption in thick glue. The caretaker has to peel this off and file each nail down individually.

Finally, he tells us he's on the last one. Mum and I step back. I remember the flood of apprehension and excitement. What will it be? I'm afraid it might be injured. I've never been good with wounded creatures.

The last nail goes suddenly and the flap comes loose with a heavy clunk that seems to startle the caretaker. He slips back and the flap falls loudly to the floor, letting loose a cloud of thick, black soot. It fills the room, covering the furniture and our faces alike. But something else emerges too.

All I can discern before the soot hits my eyes and the tears come, is a large white shape. It swoops from the chimney breast up to the ceiling and the clouding, mushrooming soot. But then I hear Mum. "An owl! It's an owl," she cries. As the soot clears from the air, I see it too, white and beautiful, a barn owl. I've only ever seen pictures of them, but I recognise its heart-shaped face as it bobs anxiously at us from the rafters. I notice how sharp its little black beak is.

Mum throws the French doors wide. But the owl doesn't move. Its head bobs. Its dark eyes dart. The caretaker tries to shoo it with his stick. It flaps a few times, showing us its huge white wingspan; the softly freckled feathers, but it won't leave.

The caretaker sees it first. Mum's hand flies to her mouth and she tells me not to look. But I follow her eyes to the small, sooty body lying in the grate, like a piece of waste packing. Exhausted and broken, feathers stuck dry with dust and ash. Dried blood around its beak, blunted claws. The chimney is very small.

We leave the French doors open all that day, but the live owl doesn't move until we carry its dead mate out to the garden and bury it. For three days, it sits in one of the dead oaks. Then on the fourth day, comes the smell of another storm; the clammy, pressured air. The owl is gone.

Only to return in these dreams. Night after night, the owls reproach me, while we wait, buried high above the earth in our own tall chimneys.

The sun hangs low now, eclipsing the stations above. The Tethers fall from nowhere, gold and ethereal. In the Senate, your discussions will be ending. An hour of peace and then the vote. I put my hands together and pray – for the first time since I was a little girl – that you will make the right decision; that something or someone will be there to help you, you and Jack, and little Luke. He has promised to bring this to you as soon as I am gone. I hope it will give you courage. We must all be night owls now.

Do not feel bad if, when you read this, you feel relief. I know, as I wait for the lift to come up, that I do. I hear the chop, chop, chop of Mum's knife on the carrots. I feel my songbook in my hand. I smell rain on the air again.

The Tethers at sunset are a sobering sight. All those trailing limbs fading into black in the deepening gloom. A herd of long-necked dinosaurs. The sun sets. The clouds of earth swirl yellow; the smog lit by the power houses below. The odd line of lightning crackles, the synapses of a dying brain.

I kiss Luke. A kiss for you too. Be bold, I tell him. I mean that for you too.

I step into the lift, and begin the descent.

Benjamin Myers

Benjamin Myers was born in Durham. His novels include *Beastings* (Bluemoose Books), *Pig Iron* (Bluemoose Books), which won the inaugural Gordon Burn Prize, and Richard (Picador), a *Sunday Times* book of the year. He recently won the Society Of Authors' Tom-Gallon Award and is a published poet. His journalism has appeared in *The Guardian, New Statesman, Caught By The River, New Scientist, Mojo* and others. He lives in Calderdale, West Yorkshire.
www.benmyers.com

A Peacock, a Pig

His legs carry him for miles in all directions until he knows every ancient pass and every cart track. Often the boy stops and stands and breathes as he watches the sky or he climbs trees to sit and listen to the birdsong and the breeze. He scales crags and boulders or lowers himself down ravines. He explores dead forests and methane-stinking moor bogs. The boy goes the places few other people go.

Alone in the hills is the only time he feels free. When school is finished and he has fed the stock and swilled out and brushed the silage into the run-off then replenished the grain barrels he takes to the wooded upper slopes to hunt and poach. He lurks and lingers. He walks the hills unheard.

The boy learns to meld and mingle to sink into the scenery; to become like a human statue or a scarecrow able to modulate his movements with his surroundings. To make himself barely recognisable to the naked eye. On weekends he walks for hours. He masters the art of stillness and silence. Of merging and blending and sinking into the soil that birthed him. Always alone.

He had only ever had one friend. One real friend.

He was gifted to him by a man. Just some man. Another working country man passing through his mother's bedroom who must have taken pity on him because as he sloped out the back door looking sheepish one day he whistled the boy over. He said: here – I've got something for you and he took him out across the yard to his flatbed where there was a large metal cage. The man lifted him up by his armpits to stand on a tow bar slick with grease.

The cage was full of piglets. They weren't pink or white like the piglets the boy was used to seeing. These ones were a shiny black; as black as the Patterdale terriers that the rat-man used when he came around to do the barn and the runs beneath the hen huts.

At the sight of boy and the man the piglets wriggled into action and wrestled with each other as if to gain their attention. They squealed and grunted and their damp noses sniffed at the air and they seemed to say to him: pick me. Pick me. Their large black ears were pressed down flat against their heads.

They're special pigs these said the man. From strong stock. A rare breed that they call a Large Black. None will grow bigger.

Then the man said: go on then lad – take any you like.

The boy looked at the man and said really? and the man said of course I've enough on my plate. Tell your Mam it's payment.

He considered the animals in their cage for a minute before he noticed a solitary pig off to one side standing perfectly still and looking in the other direction as its siblings jostled and squealed. As if seeing something in it that he recognised the boy pointed to the small black pig that was barely bigger than a can of beer.

That one he said. I'll have that one.

The man climbed up and unhooked the latch of the cage and said are you sure? It's a runt is this one and the boy nodded and said yes – that one.

The man lifted it up and swinging it to the boy by its back heels said here you go then lad.

The boy took a hold of the piglet. It was a little thing. A grunting thing. A stinking thing. It was only eight inches long; hard to believe it could grow to be big.

It's a nipper now but feed it right and you might have a giant on your hands said the man. If it makes it. The runt you can never be sure about. Vicious buggers though are the Large Black. Aggressive like. I reckon this breed got some wild boar in it way back when. Things got muddled. You'll not need a guard dog with one of them about the place.

The boy asked: what do I feed it?

The piglet was cradled in his arms like a newborn child.

Anything said the man. Feed it anything. They're not fussy. Just feed it often and feed it well. I bought the semen that made that one. I seeded the mother myself. It's one of the oldest breeds in England is the Large Black.

The man climbed up into the cab of his van and wound down the window and said to the boy aye better than any bloody guard dog and then he drove off. The truck tipped and leaned down the rutted lane and then the boy turned and ran back to the house with his new friend.

There is a girl. A classmate whose freckles make him feel dizzy. She is not the prettiest girl or the most popular girl or the cleverest but she *is* the nicest girl because once she let him hold her hand. For a few fleeting moments one breaktime when no-one was looking she and the boy made a connection.

She is a farm girl too. Like him she is clumsy and grubby and walks alone. She does not wear make-up or have many friends and she has joined the school late from another school and perhaps this is why she lets him talk to her: she is unaware of the weight of his family name.

She likes animals and she has dirt under her fingernails too and once she tells the boy that peacocks are her favourite birds because their feathers are so beautiful that they are almost unreal and to look at them is like looking at the sea from the top of a great cliff on a beautiful clear sunny day.

He has only ever seen a peacock in the books that he has thumbed his way through at school when he should be learning mathematical formulas and silly poems and facts about oxbow lakes and dead kings from a long time ago but he never forgets the look in her eyes as she says this.

One Saturday the boy is out wandering. Perhaps deep down he knows what he is looking for; perhaps he has heard rumours about people who live in another world two valleys over.

He leaves the old stone houses of the hamlet behind him and he crosses the valley. Down and across and then up. It is summer. It is humid. It has been raining for two days but the rain has stopped and now the air is close. The air is clammy and the air is tightly tuned. More rainfall will come.

He walks.

He walks without direction, purpose or intent. He is simply moving. An hour or more passes and then he is moving down a hill and through a densely wooded area. There is a stream running through it. The boy stops and stoops and drinks and it tastes beautiful. These woods are not like the woods around the village or the copses up the top end of the dale. These woods have been tended to. Maintained. Through the marshy area a boardwalk has been laid and on top of the wooden boards there is chicken wire to stop people slipping and where the path has eroded it has been fixed with flag stones. There are signs to explain which plants and animals can be found in this dell. It is a nature reserve of some sort. There is nothing like this in his valley. Only sky and scree.

The wood broadens out and takes him downhill and then the boy is leaving the trees behind and he is in a broad pasture full of buttercups with a track running through the centre of it and other tracks leading off to either side to large houses nestled in amongst trees. In his valley the houses are clustered together to form a hamlet as if by accident; a resentful huddle against the endless rain. But over here there is space. The houses have room to breathe. They have been built to blossom outwards rather than turn their back to the sun.

Even the sky seems higher.

Many of the houses look new and come with their own land and their own driveways and their own landscaped gardens featuring ponds and summerhouses and polytunnels. They have actual lawns. These lawns are tended. These lawns are not wild. They are neat. Ordered. Beside them the sunlight reflects off the large gleaming cars parked in their large driveways.

He is three or four or five miles from home but he is in another world.

Then the boy is by a big house and there is a screeching sound. The house is large. The house is huge. It has a gravel forecourt and a curved driveway and outbuildings and a walled garden. There is a big wooden electronically controlled two-door gate our front and it is open. He looks in.

The man had been right. The pig ate constantly. Its appetite knew no limit. It grew and it grew quickly.

It ate and it roamed and it followed him around like a loyal collie. And it grew.

His mother liked to prod it and cajole it. Kick it and whip it. Boot it and prod it. Always at it.

It'll help train it up tough she said. Keep it on edge. They like it like that do animals. They've got to know their place.

Soon the Large Black was dominating all the other creatures on the farm. The cats and dogs gave it a wide berth.

It ate the slops and peelings. It ate worms and bark and shoots and flowers. It ate chicken carcasses and mouldy bread. It ate rats from the rat traps and baby birds that fell from their nests. It ate dead piglets.

And it grew.

It grew to weigh six hundred pounds.

Six hundred pounds of wobbling black flesh with long lop ears framing its fat jowly face. Great teeth jutted from its lower jaw.

The pig had free run up top and when any vehicle drove up their track it wheeled and bucked and screeched a warning shot across the dale.

And his mother would give it a boot. His mother would crack it with her broom. Prod it.

Only when the boy scratched behind its ears and fed it scraps and whispered to it was the pig calmed. The rest of the time it ate and screeched and tormented every living creature who crossed its path.

It could snap and trample. Snarl and rip. Hunks of flesh would come away when he set the pig on them. Yet the pig was his salvation. The pig was his only friend.

Once one of his mother's men – a grubby mean-eyed man with a calliper on one leg – gave him a belt. A hard open-handed slap. As he reeled and howled the pig charged the mean-eyed man and knocked him flat on his back in the straw and piss. It tore through his calf muscle on his good leg like it was nothing. Lacerated him. The man screamed. The boy pointed and laughed.

The screeching is coming from around the side of the house. He hears it again. An urgent cawing. He stops: silence. The boy takes some steps up the drive way and peers round the side of the house. He walks on, aware of his feet crunching on the gravel. Around the side of the house he sees a large, beautiful peacock. A few metres away perched on the corner part of the garage roof there is another one.

He thinks of the girl and the look in her eyes and it makes his stomach flip.

The boy recognises that the peacock on the ground is a male. The boy knows this much. The one on the garage is female.

They are the most beautiful creatures he has ever seen, especially the male whose long graceful neck fades from bottle green into cobalt blue and a thousand other shades in between. When the light catches them it seems like its feathers are shimmering like a new type of fire. They are colours the boy has never seen before – more breathtaking than anything man could ever create.

The boy thinks they are other-worldly and magical. The boy is mesmerised. The boy is entranced.

He immediately knows what he needs to do.

He walks towards them and the female – the peahen – screeches again. It is less stunning but he still wants to get closer to observe it.

Though its neck has shades of blue in it too the bulk of its body is a dullish brown – charmless and flat like ditchwater. It is plumper also. Perhaps it is pregnant.

Both birds have crests atop their heads. A row of ornate feathers that spread out into delicate blue fans at the tips.

He treads carefully towards the male. He stops then squats to the bird's level. It walks from side to side and then suddenly without warning it fans out its tail feathers into their full plumage.

The boy gasps. He actually hears himself draw a tangible intake of breath that he holds in his centre.

A wall of eyes stares back at him.

The plumage is breathtaking. Literally breathtaking.

The eyes are blue in the centre but it is the shade of green that encircles them to create a mock iris that the boy is dazzled by. It is a green like no other. It is electric. It is iridescent. He can barely comprehend it.

How he wonders can such a colour be possible? How can nature create something so utterly magnificent?

The colour seems so at odds with the grey Yorkshire stone walls and the grey Yorkshire stone skies of the dales.

He has to have one of those feathers. Just one for the girl to hang from her curtain rail so that the sun can catch it in a morning and remind her that beauty exists in the world and that he did this for her.

He needs one of those feathers.

The pig was a breeder too so his mother decided he was to be seeded. The pig – she wouldn't let him name it; said that was sentimental – was put to stud.

Two men came to take it away. They hog-tied it and muzzled it and the boy protested until he got a belt from his mother but then they returned a day or two later. This began to happen often. Then when the pig was off the back of the truck the men would go indoors for a while. They'd stay with his mother a while and he would take the hog out back to give it an apple and a scratch behind those flapping ears.

And it went on. The pig coming and going and spreading its genes all over the north of England. It's reputation – like its seed – spreading far and wide.

The boy starts counting the eyes but the peacock turns away before he reaches thirty.

Hunched he walks towards it but before he can get close the peacock closes its plumage and noisily and without grace flies up to the garage roof to join its mate.

Its train of tail feathers hangs over the edge and he is amazed that such an impressive fan can fold away so neatly. Perfect colouring. Perfect engineering.

The boy turns and looks behind him back down the driveway and through the open gates. The sun is at its highest point now. The air is still close. It seems to hum.

The two peacocks survey him with suspicion from the garage roof as he first pulls gently at the plastic drainpipe to test its security and then begins to shin his way up it. He has had a lifetime of climbing up trees – fifty, sixty, seventy feet up sometimes. The drainpipe will be easy. One hand over the other.

For one feather.

Just to treasure. To study and touch.

To give to the girl to make her love him.

The birds strut across the garage roof when first the boy's head and then his torso appear beside them. One of the birds is within reach. The stunning male. He slowly stretches out an arm and counts to three then he grabs it and he feels feathers in his hands and he holds on tight and he yanks but as he does the whole section of guttering and drainpipe comes away with a splintering crack.

The boy tumbles backwards pulling the bird with him. It screeches. Both birds do. He holds on tight. With his free hands he snatches at blue sky.

The dark form of the bird blocking out the sunlight before him – above him – is the last thing he sees before blackness –

Blackness closing in and then nothing but silence.

When he comes round the sun is a lot lower in the sky and he is surrounded by black piping and feathers. Lengths and shards of shattered plastic are scattered about and small pieces of gravel are embedded in his back arms and face; his neck and head are pounding.

There is something beside him. It is the male peacock. It is crooked and it is trying to stand but its feather are jutting out at odd angles and it keeps keeling over. It can no longer tuck its plumage away and its eyes are wide with despair. It seems broken somehow.

There is a low hum in his ears. The boy feels cold and nauseous and numb. He slowly sits upright. He can barely move his neck and his vision is blurring then focusing blurring, then focusing. His jaw hurts.

He stands and the earth tilts. He takes a moment to regain his balance and then breathes deeply. He brings a hand to his lower lip and touches blood. He licks it with his tongue but it is tasteless so he brings a bloody finger to his nose and smells it. There is nothing.

The bird is still flopping about on the ground in a heap. The other peacock is nowhere to be seen. The boy goes to it and it screeches for a moment and he looks at it for a moment then it falls silent as he stamps on its neck and he stamps and stamps and then when it has stopped moving he pulls out feathers – one two three – entire handfuls of feathers – until he hears a car crunching its way up the pitted track of the house. He turns to leave and cuts across a side lawn and climbs over a fence with his jaw aching his head aching and the entire world black and white except for the feathers in his hand that capture the white sun as he runs and runs.

And then one day the two men came again and tied the pig again only this time when it came back it was vacuum packed in plastic in a hundred pieces. Porcine parts piled high.

His pig. His pal.

In parts. In pieces. He was now an *it*. A series of its.

There you go said one of the men to his mother as he slapped one of the packages down on the kitchen side. No part wasted.

You've got the brains for brawn he said.

Then we've shoulder steaks and rib racks.

Over here's what you call the hand for cubing.

These here are sides and blades for curing and hanging.

The loin for back bacon or roasting or chops.

The belly's for rolling or roasting or skinning.

Trotters for jellying or the braising of shanks.

And then there's a bucket of blood for black pudding and offal for stews and stocks.

The man still had his apron on. His hands unwashed. He looked pleased with himself.

It was old said his mother when she saw his face crumpling like a twist of newspaper thrown onto a fire. Now help get this lot inside then make yourself scarce. These boys need paying.

He gave her one those feathers. The girl with the freckles. He was off school for a week with head pains and vomiting and his sense of smell never came back but when the boy returned he had three feathers for her but by now she had made some friends; she had been accepted into a circle of boys and girls who smoked together at lunchtime round the back of that substation building near the top yard and when he approached her at dinnertime with the feathers she laughed and said right thanks and then he just stood there for a moment turning the colour of a plum while everyone tried to stifle their laughs so he turned and left and as he walked away he heard them screaming with laughter and saying things like freak and dickhead and dirty pig needs a bloody wash and when he looked over his shoulder the boy saw one of the lads whipping the feathers against the chain-link fence until the fine coloured barbs tore away from the main spine and hung in the air for a moment to catch the sunlight along with the smoke from the cigarettes that they shared as if in some ancient ritual.

The pieces of feather floated down into the dust and became part of the dust; became part of the landscape.

Part of the architecture of his failings.

Paddy O'Reilly

Paddy O'Reilly is a writer from Melbourne, Australia. She has published a collection of award-winning short stories, *The End of the World* (UQP), and her novel *The Fine Colour of Rust* (HarperCollins) was published in the UK and Australia in 2012. Her new novel, *The Wonders*, will be published in 2014 in Australia and 2015 in the USA.

Guerilla War

After Gran confiscated the porn magazine she found under Gary's mattress, he declared war. He said he was training to become a guerrilla, like the Vietnamese communists. It was 1971. Our American cousin had been sent to fight in Vietnam.

'Soldiers don't fight trench battles anymore,' Gary told me. 'I read about it. It's the new guerilla war – propaganda, ambushes, recruitment of the locals. And don't be stupid, Annie,' he warned me before I opened my mouth, 'because I don't mean monkeys.'

One night soon after, he arrived home with his mates at two in the morning. They hung around the front yard for ages, whooping like Indians every now and then, laughing. My bunk was in the room facing the yard. I lay awake listening to Gary's friends talking.

'Geez it was a runny one.'

'Did you hear it land? Splat!'

I was up early to get Dad fed and off to work. Since Mum was back in hospital, Pauline and I were supposed to take turns cooking breakfast and tea for everyone. Gary's job was to make the school lunches. The ambulance men had carried Mum out of the house on a stretcher, and all the way she kept calling us one by one and giving us instructions as she held our hands. First it was Dad, who leaned in close as she whispered in his ear. 'Of course I bloody will,' he protested loudly at one thing she said. Then we kids were each called up. Seana wasn't to eat too much. Willy had to help the babies with their schoolwork. 'They're not babies,' Willy said. We all had to wear our best clothes on Sunday for Gran's Sunday inspection. Two Sundays had passed since then but Gary hadn't turned up on either. And he hadn't made a single lunch.

When Gary got up for breakfast, I was ready to shout at him for keeping me awake but as soon as he walked into the room I burst out laughing. All over the top of his head the hair had been cut short and spiky, and lanky twists of hair snaked down the back of his neck.

'Unbelievable!' Pauline said. Gary smiled as though he thought she was complimenting him. 'What an idiot,' she added.

Gary slumped in a chair and leaned way back. 'I don't think so,' he said, smirking. He reached into his pocket and pulled out a flick knife. 'Idiots don't have these,' he said, snapping the blade open.

Pauline ran her finger down the blade. She showed us her fingertip, where a narrow white flap of skin had opened.

'They must, if you do,' she sneered.

Gary snapped the blade shut and tossed the knife into the air but Pauline caught it before him and dropped it down the front of her t-shirt, into her bra between the small mounds of her breasts. As Gary stood up and moved toward Pauline, the doorbell rang. Gran had a special way of ringing the doorbell that made it sounder louder and more aggressive than when anyone else rang it. She had been dropping in at odd times to check on us, bowling through the house on her mission of cleanliness while Pop waited outside in the car.

Pauline pulled the knife out of her bra and threw it to Gary, then ran off to our room to peel off her extra-tight jeans. Gran had already told her to give them to the poor. 'You'll ruin yourself with clothes that tight,' Gran had said as she pried her finger in between the waistband of the jeans and Pauline's stomach. 'Ruin what?' Pauline asked, pretending innocence.

The doorbell blared again.

'Quick,' I whispered, as if Gran could hear me from outside the front door, 'somebody do something.'

Gary ran his hand across the bristles of his new haircut and picked up a piece of burnt toast. I heard Seana plodding to the door.

We listened as Gran charged down the hallway toward the kitchen.

'Surprise counter-attack,' Gary said through a mouthful of toast.

'What did you say, boy?' Gran asked.

Gary shook his head. Gran pushed aside the dirty breakfast plates and slid two home-made meat pies onto the table. Then she stepped back and put her hands on her hips before looking around the room at each of us in turn, her gaze lingering on Gary a tiny bit longer.

'Dog droppings,' Gran said. Moira looked at the pies and giggled. Jimmy licked his lips and said, 'Pooh pie.'

'Don't be foolish,' Gran said and cuffed him across the head. She turned to me. 'Someone threw dog droppings through our window last night. They smashed the window with a brick, then threw in that disgusting... What a world this is becoming.'

'Oh,' I said, not looking at Gary. Nobody looked at Gary.

'What have you done to yourself?' Gran said to Gary, staring at his hair. 'You look like a hooligan.'

Gary grinned, obviously pleased.

'Where's Pauline?' Gran went on, glancing around the room. 'And Willy. Aren't they up yet?' She bustled off to the bedrooms, leaving the rest of us in the kitchen staring at the floor.

'Dog pooh? You're mad,' I whispered to Gary. He leaned back in his chair and rested his foot on the table. I stepped back, towards the sink.

'You're crazy. What if she finds out?'

'This is war,' Gary said. 'Guerilla war.'

Jimmy clapped his hands, and Gary took hold of his wrist.

'You say a word,' he told Jimmy, 'and you're dead.'

'Get your foot off that table,' Gran said when she came back, pulling Seana behind her. 'Filthy.' She slapped Gary's knee, and he slowly lifted his foot and let it drop loudly to the floor. 'Now Anne, take Seana to your room and give her something of yours to wear. Look at her, she's bursting out of these clothes. I don't know how she's got this fat.'

'I am not fat,' Seana whined.

Gran looked around the kitchen again. She seemed even more energetic than usual. 'I can't stand the way you all just loaf about. Why aren't you ready for school?'

'Because you're here,' Gary said.

'I simply did not hear that, young man. You are looking for a proper hiding.'

Gary stood up and strolled toward Gran. He paused in front of her, and leaned down a little to speak. I was holding my breath.

'Thanks for the pies Granny,' he said. He walked out of the kitchen and, even though we couldn't see, I knew from the regular metallic clicks that he was flicking his new knife open and shut.

'Seana should go on a diet,' I announced at tea time when Pauline was carving up the pies. 'Gran said so.' I had realised that morning that if Seana wore my clothes I'd be left with nothing. 'Because she's got fat,' I added.

'Yeah, you're right. She's got so fat she's got little fatty boobies,' Pauline said. 'A diet's a good idea. A strict diet.'

'Fatty,' Jimmy said, and giggled.

Moira glanced over at Seana, who refused to look up.

'I'll have the bit she doesn't have,' Willy said.

Seana waited, holding her knife and fork upright like two toy soldiers, until Pauline passed her a plate.

'Here you go fatso,' Pauline said.

On the plate were four peas, a baby carrot and a dribble of gravy and meat from the pie. I had already finished my serve. So had Willy and Gary. We all stared hungrily at Seana's plate.

'Gravy's really fattening,' Willy said. 'Seana, it's fattening. I'll have yours.'

'Who wants toast?' Gary asked, getting up from the table. He wasn't watching carefully enough. He had only just risen from his chair when Seana let fly with the plate, which frisbeed across the room toward Pauline. The peas and carrot span off the plate like planets in orbit, and Willy actually caught the carrot as it flew past his face, then stuffed it in his mouth. The plate sailed on, shaving past Pauline's ear and clipping Gary on his funny bone, until it reached the wall and smashed at exactly the time Gary yelped in pain.

'Fuck,' Gary shouted. 'Fuck, fuck, fuck.'

Seana sat still and straight in her chair, her fists clenched in her lap. I saw Moira slip her own piece of the meat pie under the table. Gary was still dancing around, screaming 'Fuck.' Pauline stood up. Seana was getting fatter, but Pauline was getting thinner, which she exaggerated by wearing skin-tight clothes. Her thin pale face and her skinny arms had always made her seem older than her age, and right now she looked like a crotchety old lady. She pointed a long fingernail at Seana.

'Go to bed!'

Seana wriggled out of the chair and ran to her room. Moira and Jimmy followed her.

'That was your fault,' Gary said to Pauline, rubbing his elbow. He turned his back to Pauline while he put four slices of bread under the griller. 'You're turning into a real bitch. You know who you remind me of? Gran, that's who. You're just like old Gran-major. You're a thirteen-year-old bag.' He laughed. 'Pauline, the old bag.'

'Hey,' she said in a voice that seemed to come from right down in her feet, 'you know who you're like, don't you. I don't even have to say it.'

While Gary pulled out the grill tray and turned over the toast, Willy sidled out of the room. I slid down under the table. From under there I could see the cracks in Pauline's shoes. I had a perfect view of her badly shaved legs and the nick just under her knee, which was crusted in dried blood. Then behind her legs was the wall, all scuffed and dented like the wall of a classroom, and on the floor the shards of Seana's plate. One pea balanced on the skirting board.

'You know, don't you?' Pauline taunted. 'Who else goes drinking with his mates and rolls in so pissed he can't remember our names? Who else besides you is so scared he runs away when Gran comes? Can you guess, Gary? I know you're stupid, but can you guess? Yeah, it's Dad. You are Dad.'

Gary dug the blade so hard into the table top that I saw its glinting tip emerge underneath where I sat. I felt like the woman who sits inside a magic box and has swords thrust through her whole body. I'd seen it happen on television. The audience laughed but I held my breath. I could imagine just how she felt. And here it was, happening to me.

'You think I'm scared of that old bitch?' he shouted, and he wrenched the knife out of the tabletop so hard that the table lifted off the ground and fell back with a thud.

The pea fell off the skirting board. Pauline's nails were clawing shreds of paint off the chair and I edged backwards, away from the end of the table where she sat and Gary stood.

'Well,' Gary said. I watched from under the table as he wiped the knife on the leg of his jeans and snapped the blade shut with his thumb. 'We'll see about that.'

Nothing happened for days. Gary hung around the house, practising his throwing against the outside toilet door. Pauline came home late every night, and one morning I noticed purple marks like bruises on her neck. Love bites, Gary called them. Slut marks, he said. He told me that night she had a boyfriend. 'But not for long,' he said. 'I'm going to get him, for making a slut out of my slut sister.'

'That's a contradiction,' I said. 'If she's a slut already, how can he make her a slut? And what exactly is a slut, anyway?'

'Your big sister,' he said. He dug the tip of his knife into the laminex of the table and twisted the blade so that a sliver of laminex curled up in a corkscrew.

'Don't,' I said. 'Look what you did the other night.' I pointed to the hole he'd made when he stabbed the table. There it was, that sensation again, feeling like I was inside the magic box with a few gleams of light filtering in through the seams of the box and someone outside sharpening the swords. 'And there, the wall all cracked, and the broken rubber on the fridge door and the burn marks on the floor. The house is falling apart.' I could imagine the tips of the sword blades sliding in through the cracks in the wall. 'We've got to fix it before Mum comes home from the hospital. It's falling apart. The whole house is falling apart.'

'It's always been like this,' Gary said.

'No,' I protested. 'It's worse. It's getting worse. We've got to do something.'

On the Sunday when Gran turned up, like she always did at nine in the morning to inspect the house and make sure we were looking after ourselves, Dad was at home. Gran sent him out to the car and he and Pop drove away. Gran lined us up.

'Where have you been these last weeks?' Gran asked Gary.

'You're not going to do this inspection thing on me anymore,' Gary said. 'I'm fourteen now.'

Gran ran the back of her hand over her forehead, then she told Gary to wait in the lounge room. She started down the line, poking our scabs and grubby collars mechanically and telling us to smarten up.

'Can we go and see Mum soon?' I asked when she got to me. 'I thought we might be going today.'

Gran rubbed her hand across her forehead again.

'Your mother's very tired, Anne. Your father and your grandfather have gone today, but she's very tired. I don't think you can go yet. I've told her that you're all fine, and I've sent your love. She's very, very tired.'

At two o'clock Gran finally went into the lounge room. Gary had been waiting for an hour. When he spoke, his voice sounded as though someone had tied knots in his throat.

I listened from the hallway.

'We're sick of you. We're not going to do what you say anymore. We don't want you coming here anymore.' His voice was getting higher as though someone was pulling the knots in his throat tighter.

'We?' Gran said quietly.

I started to shake, afraid that I might get the blame for this.

'Don't you mean just you?' Gran said.

'They're scared of you but I'm not,' Gary said.

'Now, I'm not angry with you, Gary. I know you're just a boy, a silly young boy. You need a proper father.'

'I've got a father. I don't care about him. It's you I hate.' His voice went a notch higher. 'You just come here so you've got someone to bully. The only reason you hate my father is because you can't bully him.'

This time Gran's voice went higher too. I felt pins and needles all over my body as if the voices were knives stabbing at me through the walls.

'What you've got is worse than no father at all. And the shame is that you're turning out just like him.'

There was a thud and the wall next to me shuddered. I could sense Gary on the other side of the wall, swinging his boot to kick it again.

'What can I do with you? You're so wilful. Stop damaging that wall. Stop it!' The thudding continued. 'Gary!' Gran said. 'Listen to me boy, just for once, will you listen?'

My head was all light and dizzy. I rested my cheek against the cool wall and felt the shudder as Gary's boot connected on the other side.

I leaned around the doorway to look inside. A lump of plaster had fallen out of the wall and dust was rising from the floor. Gran took a handful of Gary's t-shirt and pulled him away from the wall. She reached up, took hold of his shoulder and turned him around like a puppet.

'Look at me,' Gran said as she rummaged around in her handbag. Gary was clenching his teeth and his fists.

'You're a stupid boy,' Gran said, as she found what she was looking for in the handbag and pulled it out. 'You're a stupid boy not to see how hard I try. Look at this. Is your father in this? Is he? Is he ever here for you?' She was speaking in rhythm with her hand as it punched the air with the tatty old black and white photograph she had pulled out of her bag. Her eyes were glistening. She waved the photo around a few more times. Gary stared at the floor.

'You've got to understand that I am all you've got.' Gran stopped speaking and stepped backwards. The couch was directly behind her and she sank into it, as if her legs had deflated. She dropped the photograph on the cushion beside her. Some of her hair had crept out of the tight bun on the top of her head, and she kept trying to push it flat with her hands. I stood still, blocking the doorway. I could see the photograph sitting beside Gran.

It was one we'd all seen a million times, of Gran with all us kids crowded tightly around her. Pop said Gran carried that photo everywhere with her. In the picture, she looked as if she was floating, as if we were holding her up on a raft of people.

Gary lifted his left hand and started to bite on his knuckle. I thought Gran was about to say something. She took a breath. I waited, and Gary stayed where Gran had left him, his head bowed and his shoulders shaking. But Gran just stood up and patted her hair one more time. She slipped the photograph back into her handbag. She walked to the doorway and said as she passed me, as if she was just continuing a normal conversation, as if this was just the logical answer to some question I had asked,

'Do you see? I'm all you've got. I told her I'd look after you.'

I stepped into the lounge room and bent down to look closely at the hole Gary had made in the wall. The plaster underneath the paint was grey and crumbly, like old dirt, with hairy stuff sticking out of it. Behind the hole were slats of wood. If I could glue the broken pieces of plaster together, I might be able to stick it all back on the wood and patch the hole.

'She's not coming back,' Gary said behind me.

'Gran? Of course she is. She'll be back next week. You can't scare her away.'

Gary clenched his fist as if he was going to punch the wall, but instead he dropped his arm and sighed. As he was leaving the lounge room, he put his hand on my head like an uncle. It felt strange, as if he was sorry for me even though he was the one in trouble.

'What?' I said.

'Nothing,' he answered, and he followed Gran's footsteps out to the kitchen.

And then I realised.

Tannith Perry

Tannith Perry has lived most of her life in the US and has been writing stories since the age of five. She didn't plan on becoming a writer however, because when she was little she thought that she would end up as either the president of the United States of America or a ballerina. She studied International Development at university and has lived in West Africa, Italy and Sidmouth, England. She has worked as a freelance writer, waitress and sold haircuts on the streets of New York City. She is currently a ballroom dance instructor and working on her second novel.

All is Music

Don't assume I'm crazy just because I'm old and my skin looks like it's about to shed, and my hair is wiry and thin, and my eyes have gone all cloudy. I'm not crazy. And don't assume because you don't know me that my story is not real. Let's start at the beginning and I'll tell you the truth of how it went.

It was a regular old Tuesday. I woke up in the middle of the night from a dream of home. I dreamt I was amidst the women singing the yela, their feet packing the dirt beneath us, their hands thumping their calabashes. With throats bared to the fire, heads tilted to the stars, they sang. They sang with their full bodies because everybody knows dancing is only another way to sing. My mother was there, the most beautiful, the most graceful. Her skin so dark and smooth that without the fire she'd become the night, her eyes bright, burning stars.

I hadn't hardly thought about my mother or Senegal for years. Yet the dream was so real, the details so clear and the feeling of coming home so strong that it was a full minute after I woke before I realised the music was still playing. The drums pounded, the voices called the tune, hands clapped, as clear as anything. I must have left a radio on and fallen asleep, I thought. So I struggled up, slapping my old legs to spur them on, got to my feet, pulled on my robe and walked around the apartment. I liked to listen to the radio, gave a body some company, so I had one in every room. I walked from the bedroom to the living room, to the kitchen to the bath. All the radios were off. I was stumped for a while. Where was the music coming from? Then I had an idea. I'd heard a tale bout an old man's fillings picking up radio stations and wondered if that was the cause. Lucky for me, on the fifth floor there was a man named Mr. Sparks who'd once been a dentist. I'd go and see him in the morning. I climbed back into bed and tried to go to sleep despite the racket in my head.

The next day groggy and thick from a bad night's sleep I went about my morning routine. The elevator was broke as usual. So I had to walk two flights up, my knees aching. The air was so cold in that there hallway that I could see my breath and it made me remember back to the first time I'd breathed smoke. It was my first winter in New York. The first time I'd seen snow and ice, the first time I knew wind cold enough to steal your tears and turn them into icicles. The whole world tasted different that first year, my fourteenth year. Coming to our new country with Tata Mariama was like getting a new body, peeling off your skin, popping out your eyes, untwisting your hands at the wrist and voila! the new American me. I couldn't wait to wash off the smell of home. We even changed my name. It only took a week with my new ears to hear how wrong it sounded: Fatoumata. What did I care it was the only thing from my mother that I still had? New me was reckless and brave. New me didn't need gifts from my mother.

I pushed the button beside Mr. Spark's door and waited. The voices sang *leegi leegi ma gesu, ci li ma weesu*. It was only after he stood there and opened his mouth that I realised the problem; I couldn't hear him through the sound of the music *leegi leegi ma recu, walla sax di baaku*. He opened his mouth but my ears were pounding with the bass of the drums. "I can't hear you," I shouted. What he shouted back I don't know. But he let me come in and found me a piece of paper and a pen. I passed the story back to him and waited while he read it. Just as he looked up, a song came to the end and there was silence. "I can hear you now," I said. But as soon as the words were out of my mouth another song began. This one was different. It was called Thioro Baye Samba, sung in Wolof and it was my mother's favourite. Mr. Spark's said something but I shook my head sadly. He gestured for me to sit down and open my mouth. He smelled like bacon and old coffee and it was only then that I realised he was wearing his pyjamas. One of his hairy fingers went in my mouth and prodded around a bit. I thought, what has my life come to? A strange man wearing pyjamas with his hand in my mouth. He touched each of my fillings in turn and wrote, "Is there a change in the music?" I shook my head. Then he took his hand out of my mouth and took up the pen again. "I don't think it's coming from your teeth," he wrote. "You don't have any loose fillings or bridgework and the sound isn't affected by touch. You need to go to the doctor."

I went down the stairs disheartened. Even though I'm old, I don't make it a habit to go to the doctor. Once you start, you usually can't stop and end up dead or worse. But I went because I couldn't hardly hear myself think.

She gave me a full physical and made me strip. Then she shook her head and sent me to the ear doctor. The ear doctor tested my hearing and examined my ears. He put me in a machine and took pictures of the inside of my head or so I expect. "I don't think it's your ears," he said. "If it was a buzzing or ringing, maybe, but a repeating series of Senegalese songs? I don't think so." Then he gave me a hearing aid, which on the way home I slid into the mail slot of the old folks home down the street. If doctors can't solve your problem, they find a new problem and try and solve that.

A week passed and the music went on, looping through a series of yela songs then a handful of folk songs from the 50's. At first I tried not to listen, to distract myself with lists of grocery items and bills to be paid. I turned the TV volume up so loud that the neighbours took turns knocking on my door to complain. But nothing helped. The music played on.

I tried talking to my friends about it 'cause I was starting to get just a touch worried. But by now most of them had trouble hearing too, though of course for more usual reasons, and we couldn't have a decent conversation. They would open their mouths to tell me about their grandchild's recital and all I'd hear was the yela rhythm that mimicked the sound of women pounding grain and I'd start to tap my foot and sway my head and they'd see I was in my own world, transported by the music to somewhere they couldn't follow. And when I tried to describe to them what it was like living inside a radio that never turned off, their faces went sharp with confusion, worry, or plain outright disbelief. Soon enough I just stopped calling them.

Anyways, answering the phone was a nightmare. At first, I tried to explain to each caller, "I can't hear you because I have loud music playing in my head constantly." Looking back, I can see that this was not a good idea. A social worker showed up a week later and asked me all kinds of questions. I was getting better at lip reading and managed to be surprised at the story she arrived with. No, I don't hear music in my head, I told her. It's just that my hearing aid hasn't arrived. She left me with a handful of residential living home brochures and a squeeze of my arm. It was a close call.

After that I decided that it was safer to avoid people for a while. I took bus rides going no particular place around Brooklyn. I watched out the window at the suits and pretty people hurrying by, all the while the soundtrack and scenes from my youth played in my head. It was like mixing ketchup with peanut butter, a bizarre combination that felt wrong in your mouth. I stayed at home and watched the TV with the sound off. White girls in short skirts argued while the drums went *boom boom boom* and the voices called *"We crossed the river to find the spirits of our dead, our dead."* The commercial for laundry detergent came on and the white bear danced while the voices wailed to the sky for their lost loves and the drums went *thump thump thump.* I learned to sleep *with* the music, *inside* the music. But even after I dropped off, the soundtrack played on, the backbone for my dreams.

Eventually, even the waking world started to feel funny. I went to museums and looked at the paintings I had once loved, but alongside the melodies that held up my thoughts like a clothing line holds up clothes, none of them made sense any more. I walked up and down the main streets, peering into shop windows like I used to, but somehow the voices that called for the freedom of Africa made most of the things for sale foolish, even hateful. I realised how strange everyone's faces were; like white grub worms. Food stuck to my tongue, the flavours too alien and exotic. At that point I had to keep to white rice and tea.

It was about two months after the music began when I was sitting at the table with a bowl full of hot rice. I'd just picked up my fork when the song playing in my head suddenly got louder, like someone had spun the volume knob. I dropped the fork with a clatter and closed my eyes. It filled me to the brim, so much so that I didn't have room for any other thoughts. All was music. Waves of music, radiating spheres of music, dancing particles of music: they took me over. Without consulting my head, my body pushed itself away from the table and began to dance.

I pounded my feet and shook my hips, I fluttered my hands and rolled my head, I wiggled my shoulders and rocked my pelvis forward and back, back and forward. As I moved, my body came apart, my wrists untwisted, my eyeballs popped out, my head unscrewed, and my skin peeled away.

In this state of non-being I felt the presence of my mother and my father strong and glowing beside me. I felt their arms around me, the dust on my feet, the warmth of the sun on the back of my neck. I saw our village; a collection of concrete buildings and mud huts. I saw the pumpkin that grew from the vine on our roof the year I turned ten. I saw all the gifts I had thrown away so carelessly when I had come to America and I knew that the music was my mother's last gift to me.

Eventually I grew too tired to dance anymore and lay down on the floor. I could feel my old self had returned and knew, if I looked in a mirror, I'd see Fatoumata staring back at me. The songs grew dim and then faded away to nothing. I smiled into the silence, hearing all of its fullness and meaning.

The ambulance came for me only a day later. Must have been one of the neighbours concerned for me. But it doesn't really matter where it takes me, 'cause now I know that beyond the silence, beyond the city, beyond this tired body, the music waits, ready to take me home.

David Wareham

David Wareham studied English Literature at university, after which he undertook an MA in Creative Writing. Since then, he has always enjoyed writing poetry and short stories. Following his time as a bookseller, David taught English at a university in Turkey last year, and is currently working at the University of Warwick as a teacher to overseas students. His interests include reading, going to the theatre, and watching sport.

Nowhere Land

They have walked for three days in the stranglehold of winter. Sometimes in groups, sometimes in single file. They have slept on hard, star-lit ground and woken under coats stiff with frost. They have walked for hours at a time without talking, their heads full with pictures of tumbledown homes, of lost relatives, of the missing. Children who do not yet know they are fatherless have asked when they will see their friends again.

Hadeel tells Samah the walking has nearly ended. Samah fastens chapped hands to her mother's skirt, thinks of her empty classroom, of what remained.

They reach the crossing point. Two men at the front of the line stop, look behind them to check everybody is there. Many gulp in air as they leave the soil they can no longer trust.

They are met by people wearing blue jackets, offering their hands. They are asked their names. Only some answer. A woman says, "Everyone who knew my name is gone."

As they slip bags from numb shoulders they are offered water. Hadeel takes three sips from her bottle, hands the rest to Samah, who tips some into a cupped palm before smearing her face. They are used to steaming tea at this time of day. As she sits on the bag, Hadeel realises how little of her life is in there. She recalls how just before the shelling of their neighbourhood began, market stalls had bloomed with colour; men had idled outside shops, crimped papers held under arms like batons. Hadeel had returned with Samah from her school when the walls around them throbbed. The day after, a smoke-marbled sky suspended above them, they followed others away, stepping round bodies laid out like ripped carrion.

Samah had filled three bags, but was told one was all she could take. No room for the dancing shoes.

Every Friday evening, she would change into her dancing shoes and pinball through her house, filling each room like light. She would spin for her mother and father as they clapped, the heels of her shoes hitting the floor like clicking tongues. When she grew tired, she would wipe them to a shine, place them together under the bed, poised for their next performance.

After nearly two hours, they are told to board a truck that will take them to the camp. Hadeel and Samah sit next to a woman who breathes out angry sighs, cradling a boy whose eyes won't meet hers. Her sighs finally rest, the remaining journey left to silence. Samah is pulled from sleep by a stretch of fissured road. Hadeel kisses her forehead as her eyes open. Her skin has the taste of earth.

"When will we go back?" Samah asks her mother.

"As soon as we can," she says. "Your father asked you to be brave." Samah buries her face into her mother's neck, searching for the smell of home.

"I want to dance again," Samah whispers.

The truck descends a steep track, wheels kicking up a flare of dust. Samah looks skywards, tries to make out faces in clouds.

Hadeel glimpses the camp from above, coming into focus like a Polaroid. A vast toy town of identical homes. She pulls her daughter close.

"Is that where we will live?" Samah asks.

"For now. For now. Remember what your father said."

The truck stills. People in blue jackets are there again. This time they don't ask for names. Hadeel, Samah and the others are told to follow a man with a beard. They thread a maze of tents. Women sit cross-legged inside entrances, their faces fixed as mannequins.

They join the end of a queue tailbacked like traffic. A man in front of them has bandaged hands. His daughter flinches as the rough edges scratch her cheek.

They reach the front of the line in what seems to be a longer time than it took to drive here. Hadeel is given two blankets and one mattress.

"There are two of us," she says. "Why do we have one mattress?"

"We don't have enough. We must prioritise the children," says a woman seated at a table, her shoulders drooped like forgotten flowers. "We hope to get more supplies soon. I'm sorry." She touches Hadeel's hand, cracked as dry ground. Hadeel looks at her hand. It was the part of her that touched her husband last as he left the house with his friends, saying he must do his duty. What about your duty to me, she had thought, as their fingers unlaced.

"I will come back for you both," he had said. "Keep Samah safe. Tell her to be brave." Samah had not danced that Friday.

They are assigned a tent, and walk for another 30 minutes to what they must now call home. It has begun to snow. Samah pulls up the collar of her coat. Neither she nor her mother has gloves.

On the way, Hadeel sees no sign of a toilet or showers. She asks where they are located, and is told she will have to walk 20 minutes to reach them.

The two stand outside their tent, alone for the first time in days. Hadeel longs for her own company again. Samah waits for her mother to enter first. Hadeel takes her daughter by the hand and goes in. They stare at the blank of the floor. Hard as flagstones. They drop their two bags and the mattress. Sleet has settled like confetti on their blankets. Samah unwraps one from her shoulders, shakes it, feels its dampness in her hands.

Hadeel's head almost touches the roof as she stands up straight. She draws breath.

"This is our place for the time being, Samah." Hadeel's voice is hushed. It's the voice she uses after her daughter has been scolded by her father. Samah nods. She takes off her coat. The night air presses down on her back. She puts her coat on again.

"We should sleep in our clothes tonight," Hadeel says. "You must try to rest."

She finds the most even part of ground in the tent, moves the mattress over it. She pulls a piece of fruit from her bag, and gives it to Samah. "This will help you to feel less thirsty." Samah feels the cold juice line her throat. It does not ease her thirst.

They lie down on the mattress, draw the driest blanket over them. Hadeel kisses her daughter hard on the cheek. They shuffle closer to each other like magnets, bring their legs up to their chests in foetal balls. Outside, snow has started to rest on canvas. They hear footsteps crunch past, the muted skirl of a child.

Hadeel's body aches. On a different night from this one, she would be asleep in minutes, hand cradling her cheek, her husband's touch seeing no return. Now her eyes fix on the shadows that ghost over the tent's walls.

She is soon glad to hear the familiar timbre of Samah's breathing. She imagines she is sitting over her on that small bed where only dust now sleeps, heels brushing the dancing shoes.

By morning, snow has draped its white veil across the camp. Hadeel is woken by Samah's coughing. She sits up. Thirst hits her. She wraps the blanket tightly around her daughter.

"How did you sleep?" she asks.

"I dreamt of our house," Samah says. She coughs again. "I need to drink."

"Yes, me too."

Hadeel steps outside of the tent. Opposite, a woman peels vegetables in a bowl of water. The woman nods her head in acknowledgement. Hadeel walks over to her.

"I am new here," she says. "Please show me where I can get water."

"Do you have a container?" the woman asks.

"No. We were not given one."

The woman goes into her tent and emerges with a container.

"Please take this," she says. "I will show you where to go."

Hadeel calls Samah. They start to follow the woman, whose pace gathers. "I use this walk as exercise," she says. "It's about 15 minutes, if you're brisk."

The run of tents before them stretches as far as they can see, arranged in rows like a diagram. A wind rasps their faces. Samah's cheeks sting. The air carries a smell of burning.

Hadeel tries to memorize the route as they walk, looking for landmarks. Passing figures who loiter outside tents, Hadeel imagines if the women she sees have missing husbands, too.

"When did you come?" the woman asks Hadeel, keeping her eyes ahead.

"Yesterday."

"I have been here three months. Our village was attacked. We lost our son." She stops walking, puts a hand to her mouth. Hadeel looks away.

Close by, two girls crouch over a broken doll, its torn red arm stark on the snow.

"Most people have been kind to me here," the woman says, resuming her walk. "We are doing our best."

She glances at Samah. "Your daughter looks like you," she says. "She's pretty."

"Thank you. She has her father's eyes."

They reach the water station. Two boys stand straight as sentinels beside the taps, as if to make sure others don't waste a drop.

Though it is cold enough to see strings of breath surf the air, Hadeel bends her head to a tap, lets water roll over her face like a stream kneading its stones. It is fresh. She goads Samah to do the same, who sips from her hand as the two boys look on. Hadeel fills the container. The woman offers to carry the water, but Hadeel refuses.

"Thank you, but I must get used to this," she says.

As they move away, Samah looks back at the two boys. She catches the eye of one of them, who quickly waves.

They walk back through the grid of tents, Hadeel rehearsing the route once more in her mind.

When they arrive back at Hadeel and Samah's tent, they thank the woman.

"Keep the container," she tells them. Samah drags the container inside. The woman tugs at Hadeel's sleeve.

"I have a daughter. She goes to a school here. I will introduce her."

"That would make Samah happy. Thank you."

The woman pauses. "There are men who come here at night. They pay to take girls and women away. Don't let Samah out then."

Before sleeping, Hadeel places their bags before the entrance to their tent. She feels colder than the first night. She lets her hair fall loose over her shoulders, pulls the lids down over her bloodshot eyes. This must not defeat me, she thinks.

Hadeel is cooking. It has been five weeks since they arrived at the camp. They have been able to create some routine. They have started to explore the shops available to them. Hadeel has bought a rug; the colours are bright, and remind them of home. She has been sleeping better, feels safer in her dreams. Samah attends classes each morning, presents her workbooks to her mother as if they were trophies.

Hadeel adds water to her pan. She has only one ring of heat to use for meals. She is thankful for the warmth from the steam that clouds the tent, but sighs when she again tastes the plainness of the food. Her skin is tighter over her cheekbones.

In the corner of the tent, Samah is drawing, her hand arcing across the page.

"I need a blue pencil," she tells her mother.

"We don't have one here. I can get you one soon."

"My dancing shoes were blue," she says. "I need to colour them blue."

Hadeel brings her daughter stew and rice. "I hope it's better than last time," she says. Samah mixes her rice into the stew, takes a spoon to her mouth. Hadeel watches her.

Samah chews her mouthful quickly. "It is good," she tells her mother.

"You're lying."

"I'm not. You always cook well." She clears her plate, returns to her drawing. Hadeel's lips fracture to reveal a smile.

Samah finishes her sketch of the shoes, imagines how improved it will be with the addition of blue.

"Some of my school friends are building a snowman," she tells her mother. "They want me to help them."

"Where will you go?"

"Come with me. I'll show you the place."

Hadeel watches her daughter scoop handfuls of snow into her arms. She remembers the long summer afternoons watching Samah play outside their house, her energy outlasting the other children.

They make the head first, add a scarf which has been brought by the girl whose mother first showed Hadeel to the water station. They use two stones for the eyes. They then form the body, and place the head on top. Hadeel claps.

A boy tosses a snowball as high as he can into the air, looks at Samah.

"Catch!" he instructs.

Though she has begun to walk with a slight stoop, Hadeel lifts her head, squinting, a blind of winter sun pulled down before her face, following the snowball with Samah. Her daughter moves from side to side, spins, arms reaching up, the wishbone of her body readying itself for the catch.

It's as if she's dancing.

Judges' Profiles

Sara Davies (chair) Sara was a BBC Radio producer from 1992 to 2013, working on documentaries, arts features, poetry programmes, dramas and readings for Radio 4 and Radio 3. She has produced and Executive produced many Radio 4 series including A Good Read and Book at Bedtime, and directed around 60 Afternoon Dramas, Saturday dramas and 15' serials. She has commissioned and produced numerous short stories from many well-known and debut writers. Before working for BBC, Sara was a freelance reporter and presenter for radio (Woman's Hour, You and Yours) and television; she fronted a monthly arts programme for HTV for three years, and presented a number of social issue and arts documentaries for BBC and Channel 4. She also wrote for *The Guardian, The Observer* and various magazines. Sara won the 2014 Radio Academy Gold Award for best feature or documentary.

Rowan Lawton Rowan is a literary agent and the co-founder of Furniss Lawton – a literary agency that is part of the James Grant Group. She previously spent 10 years agenting at WME and Peters Fraser & Dunlop and represents a wide range of writers of both fiction and non-fiction. Rowan's clients include a number of debut novelists, including Emylia Hall, author of *The Book of Summers*, a Richard & Judy 2012 Book Club selection.

Sanjida O'Connell   Sanjida is a writer and broadcaster. She has had four novels published, including *Sugar Island* and *The Naked Name of Love*, and four non-fiction books; the latest two of which are: *Chimpanzee: The Making of the Film* and *Sugar: The Grass that Changed the World*. She writes on science and environmental issues for *The Guardian, The Independent* and *The Daily Telegraph*, and works as a wildlife presenter for the BBC. She has a PhD in Zoology and Psychology.

Nikesh Shukla   Nikesh is a writer of fiction and television. He is the author of *Meatspace* ('highly enjoyable' *The Guardian*) and the Costa First Novel Award 2010-shortlisted *Coconut Unlimited*. *Metro* described it as '…a riot of cringeworthy moments made real by Shukla's beautifully observed characters and talent for teen banter.' In 2011, Nikesh co-wrote a non-fiction essay about the riots with Kieran Yates called *Generation Vexed: What the Riots Don't Tell Us About Our Nation's Youth*. In 2013, he released a novella about food, called *The Time Machine*, which won best novella in the Sabotage Awards 2014. His short stories have been featured in the following places: *Best British Short Stories 2013, Five Dials, The Moth Magazine, Pen Pusher, The Sunday Times, Book Slam*, BBC Radio 4, *First City Magazine* and *Teller Magazine*. He has written for *The Guardian, Esquire* and BBC 2. He has, in the past, been writer in residence for BBC Asian Network and Royal Festival Hall.

Acknowledgments

Enormous thanks to the following people whose fantastic commitment, industry and support have made this year's Bristol Short Story Prize possible:

The judging panel – Sara Davies (chair), Rowan Lawton, Sanjida O'Connell and Nikesh Shukla. Our readers – Katherine Hanks, Lu Hersey, Tania Hershman, Richard Jones, Mike Manson, Dawn Pomroy, Ali Reynolds. Chris Hill, Jonathan Ward, Rosanna Tasker and the 3rd year Illustration students at University of the West of England. Arc Editorial Consultancy, Tangent Books, Helen Legg and Alex Holroyd at Spike Island, Mel Harris at Waterstone's, Peter Morgan and Mark Furneval at ScreenBeetle. Jane Guy and The Bristol Hotel, and Joe Burt, Annette Chown, Fran Ham, Nicky Johns, Sylvie Kruiniger, Marc Leverton, Kathy McDermott, Natasha Melia, Rudy Millard and Guide2Bristol, Dave Oakley, Thomas Rasche and especially to all the writers who entered this year's competition and gave us so much wonderful reading.